GLORY
THE CUP

THE GLORY GARDENS SERIES
(in suggested reading order)

GLORY IN THE CUP

BOB CATTELL

Illustrations by
David Kearney

RED FOX

A RED FOX BOOK 978 0 099 46111 1

First published in Great Britain by Julia MacRae and Red Fox,
imprints of Random House Children's Books

Julia MacRae edition published 1995
Red Fox edition published 1995
Reissued 2001, 2007

1 3 5 7 9 10 8 6 4 2

Papers used by Random House Children's Books are natural, recyclable
products made from wood grown in sustainable forests. The manufacturing
processes conform to the environmental regulations of the country of origin.

Set in Sabon

Red Fox Books are published by Random House Children's Books,
61–63 Uxbridge Road, London W5 5SA,
a division of The Random House Group Ltd,
in Australia by Random House Australia (Pty) Ltd,
20 Alfred Street, Milsons Point, Sydney, NSW 2061, Australia,
in New Zealand by Random House New Zealand Ltd,
18 Poland Road, Glenfield, Auckland 10, New Zealand,
in South Africa by Random House (Pty) Ltd,
Isle of Houghton, Corner Boundary Road & Carse O'Gowrie,
Houghton 2198, South Africa,
and in India by Random House India Pvt Ltd,
301 World Trade Tower, Hotel Intercontinental Grand Complex,
Barakhamba Lane, New Delhi 110001, India

THE RANDOM HOUSE GROUP Limited Reg. No. 954009

www.kidsatrandomhouse.co.uk

A CIP catalogue record for this book is available from the British Library.

Printed and bound in Great Britain by
Cox & Wyman Ltd, Reading, Berkshire

Contents

Chapter One

This is Glory Gardens C.C. before it all began. The picture was taken by my sister, Lizzie. It's not bad for her.

Back Row: Marty, Tylan, Cal, Jason and Ohbert
Front Row: Frankie, Jo, Hooker, Azzie and Erica.

That's me in the middle with the cricket bat. The one wearing the Ritchie Richardson sunhat is Azzie Nazar who's our best batsman. Our wicket-keeper with the pads on is Frankie Allen. And Calvin Sebastien is the big guy on the back row. Everyone thinks he's a fast bowler but he's not, he's an off-spinner.

My name is Harry Knight but they all call me Hooker – that's because my full name's *Harry Oliver O'Neill Knight*. Don't ask me why – ask my mum and dad. I'm the team's all-rounder and captain of the Glory Gardens Cricket XI. But I wasn't when this picture was taken.

I'll start at the beginning. You know, of course, that XI means eleven and so you may have spotted our first big problem. Only ten in the picture! But it's worse than that because Frankie's sister, Jo, is only interested in scoring and 'Ohbert' Bennett is hopeless at cricket. I mean really hopeless. That leaves eight and one of them is Erica Davies. Erica's a good cricketer – as good as any of us – and she loves playing. But some people – especially Jason Padgett – say we shouldn't have a girl in the team.

Glory Gardens is the name of the recreation ground at the back of Bason Street where most of us live; except Frankie, Jo and Jason who are from the Birdcage Estate just round the corner, and Tylan who lives in Hereward Road. We play cricket on the Rec most evenings after school in summer, and all the time in the holidays. You know, just practising and see-ing who can score the most runs. Sometimes we play three or four a side, but everyone fields. Azzie brings his dad's stumps and I've got a bat and pads and an old leather ball.

It was one evening last week, while we were playing, that we saw Kiddo Johnstone walking his fat dog, Gatting, through the Rec. He stopped and watched us for a bit. Kiddo's a teacher at Hereward Middle School, where we all go. We call him 'Kiddo' because that's what he always calls us. He used to play county cricket before he injured his knee and started teaching. He still walks with a bit of a limp. Azzie's dad, who knows everything about cricket, says he was a pretty good bat and a medium-pace seam bowler.

Kiddo's all right really – as teachers go. He goes on a bit when he starts telling stories about things that happened to him aeons ago. But, as most of his stories are about cricket, we don't mind too much.

After he had watched us for nearly half an hour, Kiddo came over.

"That wasn't bad, kiddoes," said Kiddo. "Ever thought of forming a team?"

"Yeeeah!" said Frankie, going into one of his daft, wild war dances which we always ignore completely. Kiddo gave him a strange look. We all know Frankie's a bit bonkers – but that's another story.

There are no organised cricket teams at school. We play softball cricket in P.E. now and again but that's all.

"How? Who'd we play against, Mr Johnstone?" asked Cal.

"Well, I was thinking – if you're keen, that is," said Kiddo. We all nodded. "Well, I've been wondering if it wouldn't be an idea to set up an Under Eleven side at The Priory. It's time we brought some younger players into the club."

"You bet," said Frankie and he started practising imaginary hooks for six over square-leg.

Eastgate Priory C.C. is one of the best clubs around. They have their own ground and pavilion just down the road, at the end of Woodcock Lane. Kiddo opens the batting for the first team.

"But we haven't got eleven players," said Marty Lear, who always looks on the black side of things.

"How many have you got, kiddo?" asked Kiddo.

"Nine," I said quickly before Marty could speak. There were a few gasps of amazement but I don't think Kiddo noticed anything.

"That sounds all right for starters," he said. "I'm sure we can find another couple of players. Tell you what, I'll ring a few people at the Club and give you the verdict at school tomorrow. By the way, who's your captain?"

"Hooker is," said Cal pointing at me and no one argued.

"Good," said Kiddo. "See you tomorrow then, Harry."

And off he went with Gatting waddling and puffing along beside him.

"Nine!" snorted Marty Lear after Kiddo was out of earshot. "Where do you get nine from?"

"Eight plus Ohbert," I said.

"Oh but, Hooker . . ." began Ohbert (that's why we call him Ohbert).

"You'll have to play until we find someone better," said Cal.

"Shouldn't be hard," said Tylan. Everyone, except perhaps Ohbert, knew that Ohbert was seriously awful at cricket, and virtually everything else, too.

Ohbert's like a creature from outer space. When he says something, people just look at each other and shrug their shoulders. No one has a clue what he's talking about. He's quite short and weedy and he grins a lot, especially when he's on his own. He always wears a baseball cap, usually back to front. Cal says it's his head that's on the wrong way round.

"Erica can't play," said Jason suddenly.

"Why not?" asked Erica.

"Well *I'm* not playing in a team with girls in it," said Jason.

"Just because she's better than you," said Azzie smiling at Erica.

"Don't be ridiculous," said Jason and he stormed off. But we knew he'd be back.

———————●———————

That evening, Cal and I were sitting in my room trying to work out the team and batting order for our first game. This is what we finally came up with (in batting order).

Hooker Knight (capt)	Tylan Vellacott
Jason Padgett	Marty Lear
Azzie Nazar	Ohbert Bennett
Cal Sebastien	A. N. Other
Erica Davies	A. N. Other
Frankie Allen (wkt)	Scorer: Jo Allen

I was used to making up cricket teams with Cal. We'd spend hours selecting the 'best England team', 'best West Indian team', 'best cricket team of all time' and so on. But it was strange to be working on our own team.

Cal's a lot taller than me and he's the strongest in our class by miles. But though he's big I've never seen him take advantage of his size and push anyone around. Mind you, he's got a terrible temper, but even when he goes really wild he just shouts and screams at you and then in a couple of minutes he forgets all about it. We've been best friends since his family moved into Bason Street. Apart from being nearly as mad about cricket as I am, he's a good laugh.

"The batting's not too bad," said Cal. "At least it's okay down to Erica."

"Do you think Jason'll play if Erica's in the team?" I asked.

"Yeah, as long as you let him open the batting with you and people don't keep telling him she's better than he is," said Cal.

"Who do you think should open the bowling with Marty?"

"Dunno. 'Spose it'll have to be you again," said Cal. He grinned. "Proper Captain Marvel, aren't you – opening bat and bowler!"

We both knew we badly needed another bowler. Marty's quite fast, but I'm only medium-pace. And we've only one other bowler we can rely on to take wickets – that's Cal with his off-breaks. Erica and Tylan are okay but I really hoped Kiddo would find us someone as quick as Marty – or even quicker.

The door burst open. "What're you two doing?" said Lizzie barging in. My sister can't stand not knowing everything that's going on.

"Clear off, stupid," I said but she'd already grabbed our team list.

"What's this? Don't tell me. Boring cricket again. When are you ever going to grow up?" She took another look at the list. "Hello, 'Hooker Knight (capt)'. What's this, then? What a joke – is my dearest brother going to be the captain of a cricket team?"

I kicked her on the shin, pulled the team sheet out of her hand and pushed her giggling out of my room.

"Boring cricket, boring cricket," she chanted outside the door.

Cal and I shrugged. He's got a younger sister, too, so he knows what it's like.

———————— • ————————

Next morning, Cal and I saw Kiddo as soon as we walked into the playground.

"It's on, kiddoes," he said. "You're the official Eastgate Priory Under 11 Team. And I think I've found you a couple of extra players, too."

He seemed quite excited and Cal and I looked at each other. We knew Kiddo was taking a big gamble with us and we both hoped we were up to it. Then he dropped the bombshell.

"Your first game's against Wyckham Wanderers. I think they're quite useful so it'll give us a chance to see what you're like. Can you arrange for your team to be at the Priory Ground on Wednesday, Harry? It's a twenty overs a side match; five o'clock start."

12

Chapter Two

"They're in the Under 11 Area League *and* Wyckham Firsts won the County Cup last year," said Marty. "We're going to get stuffed."

I didn't need telling that Wyckham was one of the strongest clubs around. They had Under 11, Under 13 and Under 15 sides as well as their Firsts and Seconds at senior level.

"But we've got Ohbert on our side," said Frankie. "That'll make all the difference."

"Bet I score more runs than you," said Ohbert who was listening for a change.

"Tell you what, Ohbert," said Frankie. "I'll give you 50p for every single run you score."

"Oh but . . . all right then," said Ohbert with a silly grin.

We laughed. The chances of Ohbert scoring a run were about three zillion to one.

We were making our way along Woodcock Lane to the Priory Ground for our first game. Everyone had heard some story or other about the brilliant Wyckham Wanderers and none of them were good news for us. As we walked along we were getting gloomier and gloomier.

Finally, Jo Allen said, "I don't care how good they are. Glory Gardens can beat anyone if they want." No one looked very convinced but it was good to have one fanatical supporter.

"I hope the players Kiddo's found us are world class," said Cal.

"And I hope they won't mind playing in a girl's team," said Jason.

"Oh, give it a rest, Jacey." Cal was getting really fed up with Jason whining on and on about Erica. None of the others seemed to think it was a problem having her in the team, except perhaps Frankie, but I was still feeling a bit bothered about it. I was pretty sure that there'd be no girls playing for Wyckham, or any of the other Under 11 teams for that matter. And I'd never actually told Kiddo she was playing.

I needn't have worried. When we arrived at the ground Erica was already there. She'd arrived already changed and was talking to Kiddo and two other boys.

"Ah, Harry," said Kiddo. "Here are your two players: Matthew Rose and Trevor Collinge."

I said hello and at that moment the opposition arrived in a yellow minibus with 'Wyckham Wanderers Cricket Club' printed on the side of it. We watched them as they got out. They seemed big. A lot bigger than all of us – except for Cal. And they were all wearing white cricket gear and carrying cricket bags.

We must have been staring at them because one of them said, "What are you lot looking at? Never seen a cricket team before?"

"Oh, they're a cricket team," said Frankie. "We thought you'd come to paint the pavilion."

I had a nasty feeling we weren't going to look much like a cricket team when we got changed. I turned to Matthew and Trevor, "Can you bowl?"

"Oh, yes," said Trevor.

"No," said Matthew.

We were in trouble. The game was twenty overs a side and the rule is that no bowler can bowl more than four overs. That meant I had to have at least five bowlers. Marty, me, Cal bowling his very slow off-breaks, Trevor and who else? Tylan perhaps, but he wasn't very accurate and he'd probably give away a lot of wides. Erica was straighter but she was in the

14

team for her batting not bowling. I decided to bat if I won the toss.

I lost and they chose to bat first. So we were in the field.

After we'd changed, Jo came over with a brand new score-book Kiddo had given her. She'd filled in the top of the first page like this.

HOME TEAM GLORY GARDENS	v WYCKHAM WNDRS.	AWAY TEAM	AT EASTGATE PRIORY DATE MAY 19TH
INNINGS OF WYCKHAM WNDRS.		TOSS WON BY W.W. WEATHER GOOD	

"Aren't we called Eastgate Priory today?" asked Azzie.

"Not if I'm scoring," said Jo. "My team's called Glory Gardens."

"I'll talk to Kiddo about it," I said. But somehow I never got round to it. I had other things on my mind – bowlers and field placings, for a start. I told Jo that Marty and Trevor were going to open the bowling and she wrote their names down on the scoresheet.

All the team – apart from Frankie who was still trying to find his wicket-keeper gloves – were out on the pitch, throwing around my old leather ball. Everyone except Tylan and Ohbert were, at least, wearing white shirts. Frankie and Marty were in their grey school trousers; Erica wore white tennis shorts. Azzie, Trevor, Matthew and I had proper cricket trousers. Cal had found a pair of trousers belonging to his brother which were nearly white and his mother had somehow made them fit him because his brother's two years older than him and quite fat. Tylan wore jeans, a yellow tee-shirt and black trainers. Ohbert had decided on a purple sweatshirt with green palm trees on it and a pair of baggy shorts; at least they weren't his most colourful ones. Wyckham looked like a proper cricket team; we looked as if we were going to play on the beach.

I let Marty and Trevor know they were bowling and started telling everyone where to field. I'd learnt all the field positions from a book Azzie's dad had lent me. It didn't help much to begin with because half the team didn't know what I was talking about. When I told Ohbert to go to mid-off he looked quite upset and started to leave the field. So I gave up and just pointed to the positions instead.

Marty's a good, straight bowler; quite quick for his height. So I decided on a fairly attacking field to start with – including two slips. It nearly paid off.

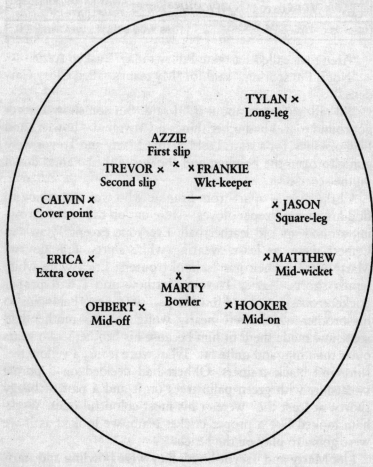

This is the field I set for Marty's first over. I'd planned the positions before the match because it's easy to get confused

16

when you've got nine fielders to think about. There's only one
player on the boundary, two slips and the rest form a ring
around the bat, saving singles. To score, the batsmen have to
hit through or over the ring.

In came the two umpires – grey-haired, wheezing Sid
Burns, the regular Priory umpire and a serious and very
smartly-dressed Wyckham offical. He went to square-leg
where he kept looking across at Ohbert's shorts, frowning
and blowing his nose on a big white handkerchief. Ohbert
didn't notice anything as usual; he was watching Gatting
rolling in something in front of the sight-screen.

Both their openers looked good. You can tell good cricketers just by the way they walk to the wicket and take guard.
"Middle and leg," said the taller of the two in a rather posh
voice, and he faced up to Marty.

At last we were ready and Marty ran in to bowl. His first
ball was a wide. The second was straighter and the batsman
swung outside the off-stump and got an edge. It flew to Azzie
in the slips, low and hard to his left and he dropped it. Marty
looked furious. His next delivery was a fast full toss down the
leg side. The batsman missed; it bounced in front of Frankie
and popped over his head. Four byes.

5 for none and they hadn't scored a run with the bat yet.

"Slow down a bit and get it straight," I said to Marty. He
huffed and puffed a bit but his next four balls were pretty
good and only one run came off them.

Now it was Trevor's turn.

His first ball pitched half way down the wicket and the tall
batsman took a great swing at it as it bounced for the second
time under his bat. Frankie stopped it on the fourth bounce
and grinned at me.

I thought, Oh no, he can't be as bad as that.

The next was a high full toss. It was looping and very slow
– much slower than the batsman thought – because he ducked
and the ball lobbed over his head, hovered a little and then . . .

17

it landed right on top of the bails, shattering the stumps everywhere. The tall batsman looked at the demolished wicket and walked off shaking his head.

Azzie and Frankie took one look at each other and collapsed on their backs screaming with laughter.

"Was it a Scud missile?" asked Cal.

"Or a UFO?" said Tylan.

Trevor looked at them crossly and mumbled, "It must have slipped."

Frankie was still smirking at Azzie behind his gloves when the next man came in. He was Wyckham's captain; Liam Katz was his name.

Azzie came over to me. "This is the one," he said. He'd told me before the game that one of the Wyckham team was a brilliant bat. "Their umpire says he's played six times for the County Colts Under 11s."

"We'll have to get him out quickly, then," I said without much confidence. I didn't like to think what he'd do to Trevor's bowling.

The first ball he received bounced half way down the pitch, he left it. The next was nearly as short and it went for four, miles over Ohbert's head. The fifth ball was a full toss which Liam pushed out on the off-side. But the shot was so well timed it raced between the covers. It should have been only two runs but Jason fell over picking the ball up and his throw was so hopeless they ran three.

I put Erica out on the square-leg boundary and moved Azzie out of the slips. Trevor bowled another long hop to the second opener who had so far only faced one ball. He swung it in the same direction as Liam's four, but this time Erica was under it. She ran in about ten yards and took a brilliant catch.

"Great catch!" cried Cal. I noticed Jason scowling.

"And outrageous field placing, too," said Tylan. "Or was it outrageous luck?"

I grinned.

"Well bowled," said Frankie rushing up to Trevor and

18

Erica catches the ball high so that her eyes can watch it right into her hands. She uses the 'baseball' style of catching with fingers pointing up and palms facing the ball.

patting him on the back. Tylan and Cal laughed but Trevor wasn't amused.

As the fielders changed over at the end of the over I saw Jason say something to Frankie. I didn't hear what it was but immediately Erica turned on him, "What the hell's the matter with you, Jason Padgett. No one else minds about me playing for this team."

"You should stick to netball or rounders," said Jason.

Erica turned away. "Oh, I've had enough of this!" she said and I think she would have walked off if Cal hadn't gone over and had a quiet word. I should have told Jason to keep his remarks to himself but I had Trevor to think about.

13 for two after two overs and we were bowling rubbish – or, at least, Trevor was. What was I going to do? He was almost as bad a bowler as Ohbert – but he had taken two wickets. Take him off or leave him on? I decided to risk it.

Marty's next over went for five runs, all singles. He was bowling sensibly and straight but Liam seemed to be able to score singles anywhere he wanted.

All too soon, Liam was facing Trevor again. Two full tosses both went for fours past cover point. The next was a wide – a full toss miles over the batsman's head! Then another wide down the leg side which Frankie stopped brilliantly, diving to his left.

I could hardly bear to watch. Two; four; then a screaming drive into the covers which Azzie stopped and saved a certain four and, finally, two more off another full toss.

18 from the over; the score had leapt up to 36 for two after only four overs. I'd made the wrong decision all right keeping Trevor on and everyone knew it.

Marty got me off the hook next over. He bowled the batsman at the other end with his second ball, knocking back the off-stump. That brought in their wicket-keeper, a spotty, round-faced boy called Charlie Gale.

But who was I going to bowl next? Cal, Erica or me? We'd all have to bowl four overs now. I threw the ball to Cal. He grinned. "Time for some real pace, is it?" he said, loud enough for the Wyckham players to hear.

"Thanks, er, well bowled," I mumbled to Trevor – not meaning it but thinking that he might need cheering up.

I couldn't believe it when he turned on me and said, "Two wickets and you get taken off. Call that fair?" He was almost in tears.

Cal took a long run up and then bowled one of his very slow, looping off-breaks. Liam was taken by surprise and played the shot hopelessly early. He hit the ball well enough but it went straight up in the air.

"Mine!" screamed Azzie.

It wasn't – it was definitely Frankie's catch. He was right under the ball and I watched in horror, unable to open my mouth, as Azzie piled into Frankie from the front and Jason, who'd decided it was his catch, too, collided with them both from the side just at the moment that the ball hit the keeper's gloves. All three collapsed in a pile with Frankie on the bottom and Jason on top. The ball shot up out of Frankie's gloves and landed on the highest point of the heap. Very slowly it ran down Jason's back, over Frankie's bottom and dropped to the ground. Meanwhile the batsmen ran an easy single.

"You idiots!" cried a muffled voice from the bottom of the tangle of bodies. "It was the keeper's catch."

"I called for it," said Azzie.

I knew I should have shouted for Frankie to take the catch. I was in the perfect position to see it all but I hadn't been able to get the words out in time. Maybe I shouldn't be captain; I didn't seem to be very good at it. We'd let them off the hook. They should have been 36 for four. Instead they were 37 for three and Liam was still there, batting brilliantly.

You can see the problem we had from Jo's scoresheet.

HOME TEAM GLORY GARDENS	V WYCKHAM WNDRS.	AWAY TEAM	AT EASTGATE PRIORY DATE MAY 17TH	
INNINGS OF WYCKHAM WNDRS.		TOSS WON BY W.W.	WEATHER GOOD	
BATSMAN	RUNS SCORED	HOW OUT	BOWLER	SCORE
1 A.WOOD	1.》	bowled	COLLINGE	1
2 R.RAWLINSON	》	ct DAVIES	COLLINGE	O
3 L.KATZ	4.3.1.1.1.4.4.2.4.2.1			
4 B.TATE	1.1.》	bowled	LEAR	2
5 C.GALE				

After you've written down
runs scored, you put a dot.

This means the batsman is out.

21

Liam had already scored 27 out of their total of 37.

To make things worse the next ball from Cal had Charlie Gale plumb lbw playing back right in front of his stumps, but the Wyckham umpire shook his head and said, "Not out" in a squeaky voice. Cal wasn't pleased but he finished a really good over and then Marty bowled his last for three runs. He ended his spell with good figures – this is what it looked like in the score-book.

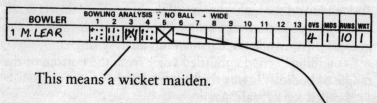

This means a wicket maiden.

This marks the end of a bowling spell.

I decided to bring myself on to bowl at Marty's end. I'm about medium-pace, as I've said, but, maybe I didn't tell you, even though I bat right-handed, I bowl left-handed. Bowling's one of the few good things about being left-handed. Sometimes right-handed batsmen find it more difficult to face left-arm bowlers because of the way the ball is angled across them.

Cal and I bowled six overs for only 16 runs – partly because Liam Katz wasn't facing much of the bowling, but also because we bowled well. I was pleased they weren't scoring so fast, but we needed wickets, too. They were 58 for three after 13 overs.

When Cal had bowled his four overs I decided to replace him with Erica. She immediately had a big shout for lbw against Liam turned down by the Wyckham umpire. But soon Liam got the hang of her bowling and the runs seemed to be coming faster and faster.

I had one more over left to bowl but I decided to keep that for the end of the innings; so I asked Tylan to have a go at bowling his leg breaks. He bowled really well with only one wide in his first over and one or two balls turned quite a lot. Sometimes it's easier to score runs off the quick bowlers than the slow ones.

Liam got a four off the first ball of Erica's next over but then he started playing very strangely. He played and missed a couple of times and seemed unusually jumpy. Finally, he pushed the last ball of the over straight to Azzie at extra cover and screamed for a single. Azzie picked up on the run and threw straight and hard to the bowler's end. Erica caught the ball and whipped off the bails. Out! Run out by a yard.

"Hard luck, Liam. 49," someone shouted from the boundary.

"I know," said Liam, shaking his head sadly. No wonder he'd been nervous. He'd missed his 50 by one run. We clapped him in; it had been a brilliant innings.

Next in was Winford Reifer. I knew Win from football practice. He's a good footballer and he'd told me he was a really fast bowler. We'd soon find out.

He batted left-handed which caused all sorts of problems for me because I had to keep changing the fielders round every time the batsmen changed ends.

With four overs to bowl, they were 71 for four. If we could hold them to 90 we still had a chance.

Tylan bowled to Charlie the wicket-keeper. Bang. Straight over mid-off's head for three. I was fielding right out on the boundary to the left-hander and no one could hear my instructions from there. Jason dropped an easy catch and Frankie missed a stumping chance – both off Tylan.

Wyckham were starting to score singles everywhere and we were running all over the place.

"I thought we were playing cricket, not doing a sponsored walk," said Marty gloomily as he trudged from one end of the pitch to the other at the end of an over.

I came back on to bowl my last over. The first three balls of it went for seven runs, including a huge four by Reifer which bounced once just inside the boundary – another couple of yards and it would have been a six. I should have left Tylan on, I thought to myself. Then, next ball, Win Reifer took another huge swing and missed. His middle stump kicked back. Out! The next batsman lasted one ball; a swing outside the off-stump and – snick – Frankie took a good catch behind the stumps. One ball left and I was on a hat trick.

I brought all the fielders in close.

"Bowl him a yorker," said Cal, handing me the ball. I tried to but only succeeded in bowling a full toss. The batsman swung hard. Everyone ducked. Suddenly, I saw the ball coming straight to me. I put up my hands to protect my chest and there was a loud cheer. I looked at my hands and the ball was resting between them. I couldn't believe it. I'd got a hat trick!

"Brilliant!" yelled Cal, running up to congratulate me.

"Great ball," said Frankie with a smirk. "Nothing like a surprise full toss."

I didn't care. Everyone knew I'd been a bit lucky but they were all really excited. I'd got a hat trick in Glory Gardens' first game.

Trevor spoilt the celebrations a bit. "Dead jammy!" I heard him say.

Erica's last over went for just four. She had another good shout for lbw turned down by the Wyckham umpire and he also gave two ridiculous wides. Charlie Gale was run out going for a run off the last but one ball.

They finished on 92 for eight. It was a good score, but it could have been a lot worse for us.

"Not too bad for beginners," said Cal as we walked off. "What do you think about that umpire, though. I reckon he was cheating."

I'd been wondering about that, too.

Chapter Three

As Matthew and Jason walked out to bat, Kiddo and I were looking at Jo's scoresheet. Gatting kept trying to look too, but he smelled horrible and Kiddo pushed him away.

I couldn't believe we'd kept them to 92 for eight. We'd had some luck all right, especially Trevor's two flukey wickets but we'd dropped three catches and the fielding had been a complete joke at times.

"That was a pretty good innings," said Kiddo, pointing at Liam's score. "I'm rather sorry he missed his 50."

I wasn't. But it didn't seem very sporting to say so.

"We should have got him out earlier," I said. "If only I'd called for Frankie to take that catch."

"Don't be too hard on yourself, kiddo. I've seen dafter pile-ups in Test Matches," said Kiddo.

"It's a big total."

"Yes. But I reckon you all did well to hold them to that," said Kiddo. "They're a good team and you're only just getting going." He looked up from the scoresheet. "Oh, by the way, I'm sorry about young Trevor Collinge. His dad told me he was a cricketer. Sometimes dads don't see things quite straight, do they?"

I smiled but I was wondering where Trevor had got to. I hadn't seen him since we came off the field.

Jason was about to face the first ball of the Glory Gardens innings. I hoped I'd got the batting right. Matthew said he preferred to open and I was happy to bat at six. So this was

25

the batting order which Jo wrote in the score-book.

J. Padgett	F. Allen
M. Rose	T. Vellacott
A. Nazar	M. Lear
C. Sebastien	T. Collinge
E. Davies	P. Bennett
H. Knight	

We soon discovered that Matthew could bat, which was a relief. He wasn't flashy and he didn't take chances. You could even call him boring but he played straight and that's what we needed. Win Reifer opened the bowling and he was really quick. His second ball hit Jason on the arm. Jason dropped his bat and fell writhing to the ground.

"There's a big brave boy," I heard Erica say quietly to herself. Jason always made a huge fuss when he got hurt. The next ball from Reifer was again short and Jason backed away and then stuck out his bat. The ball took a top edge over the slips for four and Win glared down the wicket at him. Win Reifer was at least a yard faster than Marty and because he was tall he got the ball to bounce a lot. Matthew seemed to be playing him calmly enough but Jason didn't look as though he was going to last very long.

Sure enough, in Reifer's second over he got a thin outside edge playing back to a short ball with his bat miles from his body and Liam Katz at first slip took a good catch.

We were 9 for one.

Azzie was next in. Like a lot of short players he just loves quickish bowling and he soon had the score moving along. He played one beautiful hook off a short ball from Reifer and it crossed the boundary before any of the fielders could move. Then, as sometimes happens with Azzie, he got careless and swung loosely across a well-pitched-up ball and he was out lbw, plumb in front of his stumps. We were 24 for two after six overs and our best batsman was gone.

*Jason plays back to a
short-pitched ball but his
bat is a long way from his
body and he is stepping
backwards.*

*This is how he should have
played the shot – with his
elbow high and his eye
behind the ball. Look at
the position of the feet in
both pictures.*

In came Cal. On his day, Cal's almost as good as Azzie. He's
not such a natural cricketer but he sees the ball quickly and
because he's big and strong, he hits it really hard. Sometimes
he's a bit of a slogger but he can play straight when he wants.
Today he'd obviously decided to get on with it.

His first ball from Win Reifer was short and he pulled it for
four. Then he played two powerful straight hits off the other
opening bowler.

35 for two after eight overs. We weren't doing badly. They'd been 43 for three after eight but they didn't have a bowler like Trevor . . . And where was Trevor? I hadn't seen him since the end of the Wyckham innings.

Liam Katz came on at the same end I'd bowled from. He bowled medium-pace off a short run. Cal welcomed him with a straight drive back over his head for two.

You could see Cal getting more and more confident with every ball. He faced the last ball of Liam's over. It was well pitched-up and Cal took a big stride out of his crease and drove. He missed. The ball bounced off his front pad and the wicket-keeper and bowler appealed. Up went the umpire's finger.

Cal stared back at the umpire in disbelief. He said something I couldn't hear but we all heard the Wyckham umpire.

"Don't you understand, boy? I said OUT!" he squeaked. And he stood there with his finger still held high. Cal walked off slowly.

As he passed us, he was bursting with anger. "Blind creep! Couldn't he see my foot was miles down the pitch AND outside the off-stump."

When he reached the changing room we heard an enormous crash.

"There goes the cricket bat," said Frankie. There were a few grins. Everyone knew what Cal was like. He had a hell of a temper. But he'd calm down soon enough. I wasn't too happy, though because I'd lent him my bat.

"Something tells me that umpire's playing for them," said Azzie.

"Either that or he needs specs," said Frankie. "What's his name, Jo?"

Jo looked at her scoresheet where she'd written down both the umpires' names. "F. Whitehouse," she said.

"More like White Stick," said Frankie. "I wonder what the F stands for? Fiddler?"

"No, Fingers," said Tylan. "I've never seen an umpire so

28

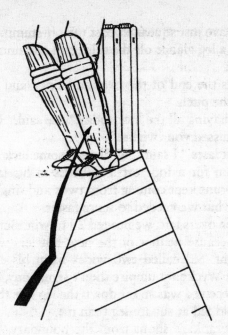

Was Cal out? If the ball hits his pad outside the line of the off-stump and he is playing a shot he can't be out lbw.

keen to put his finger up."

"Only when *we're* batting," said Marty gloomily.

Erica and Matthew played sensibly for a time, pushing singles here and there.

Then Matthew got a horrible shooter from Liam Richards which hit the bottom of his middle stump and I was in.

"Hard luck," I said as I passed Matthew on his way back. "That was a really good innings." I meant it, too. He'd scored 12 – all in singles – off 12 overs. Pretty slow, but he'd held up one end well while others had scored the runs.

I was feeling very nervous. I took guard – middle and leg – and glanced round the field. I had a good long look at the score-board while I tried to concentrate. 47 for four and we were in the thirteenth over. Just as well I'm not superstitious.

I missed Liam's first two balls completely and the second

one must have just squeaked past the off-stump. I got off the mark with a leg glance off the third ball and immediately felt a lot better.

That was the end of the over and Erica and I met in the middle of the pitch.

"You're having all the luck today," she said. "I don't know how that missed your wicket."

"I hope it lasts," I said. "We'll need some luck to win this."

I hit Liam for a four off a full toss in his last over, but mostly the runs kept coming from twos and singles. We were going okay but we needed to score faster.

With four overs left, we needed 29 to win. But we still had a chance because neither of the new bowlers were bowling very straight. Sid called two wides from his end but sure enough the Wyckham umpire didn't signal any, even though one ball I received was so far down the leg side that it seemed nearer to old Sid at square-leg than me.

I heard Frankie's shout from the boundary, "How many wides was that, Umpire?"

Two balls later, Erica got one going well down the leg side and swung at it. She missed and I think it must have brushed her pad on the way through to the keeper. "Owzthat!" The keeper appealed, followed, a second or two later, by a feeble appeal from the bowler. It obviously wasn't out; her bat had been miles away from the ball.

"OUT!" Up went the Finger. Erica turned and walked without looking at him. I couldn't believe it and I stared at Fingers but he looked away. The Wyckham players all gathered round Charlie the wicket-keeper talking in whispers. You could tell they didn't think it was out either.

Frankie didn't bother to take a guard. He swung at his first ball and it squirted down to long-leg for one. He played the same shot to the next ball he received and was caught at mid-wicket.

Tylan isn't much of a batsman, so I didn't know whether to tell him to block the ball or have a go. In the end I said nothing. I think I must have still been dazed by Erica's dismissal. Tylan hit his first ball to mid-off and called for a single. It was a short one to say the least but I ran. Tylan was running to the danger end and Liam's throw hit the stumps. He was out by at least two yards.

We had gone from 66 for four to 67 for seven in four balls.

"No chance now," said Marty, arriving at the wicket. Typical Marty. But, to be fair, scoring 26 off 16 balls was going to take a miracle.

I drove the next ball, a half-volley, through the covers for two. The one after was a similar ball but wider. I swung and got a very thin edge. I turned and saw the ball dropping into the keeper's gloves. I started the long walk back almost before they could appeal.

I looked up and saw Ohbert coming towards me, padded up.

"Where's Trevor?" I said.

"I think he's gone home," said Ohbert. "Oh but, don't worry, Hooker. We'll get the runs."

What a joke. Ohbert was worse than useless. He'd only just worked out which way up to hold the bat. None of us really knew why he kept turning up to play at Glory Gardens. He was so useless even Jason could bowl him out nearly every time. And he looked ridiculous with the top of one pad stuck up his shorts.

The first ball, amazingly, hit his bat – probably because he hadn't seen it or wasn't looking – and Marty called for a run. It was a close call because Ohbert got his bat tangled up in his pads and nearly fell over, but they made it.

"Oh, no, I don't believe it. That's 50p," said Frankie.

The end came predictably. Marty played out the over and then it was Ohbert's turn to face. He couldn't hit two in a row, could he? The bowler ran in and Ohbert started to stroll down the wicket. As the ball passed him, there was a flurry of pads and bright-coloured shorts. The bat missed its target by a good eighteen inches and swung over Ohbert's head, carrying Ohbert with it. He landed flat on his back with his legs in the air and at least three yards out of his crease.

Charlie the keeper had time carefully to lift off the bails with the ball in his other hand. Stumped.

We'd lost by 21 runs. 71 all out.

INNINGS OF WYCKHAM WNDRS......... **TOSS WON BY** W.W. **WEATHER** GOOD.

BATSMAN	RUNS SCORED	HOW OUT	BOWLER	SCORE
1 A.WOOD	1·	bowled	COLLINGE	1
2 R.RAWLINSON		ct DAVIES	COLLINGE	0
3 L.KATZ	4·3·1·1·1·4·4·2·4·2·1·1·1·1· 4·1·2·1·2·2·2·1·4	RUN	OUT	49
4 B.TATE	1·1·	bowled	LEAR	2
5 C.GALE	2·1·2·3·1·1·3·1·1·1·1·	RUN	OUT	17
6 W.REIFER	1·1·1·2·4	bowled	KNIGHT	9
7 T.WOOD		ct ALLEN	KNIGHT	0
8 H.PARKIN		c & b	KNIGHT	0
9 G.BURGESS	2·	NOT	OUT	2
10 P.PRESTON		NOT	OUT	0
11				

FALL OF WICKETS												BYES	4·		4	TOTAL EXTRAS	12
SCORE	6	13	36	71	88	88	88	90				L.BYES	1·		1	TOTAL	92
BAT NO	1	2	4	3	6	7	8	5				WIDES	1·1·1·1·1·1·		7	FOR WKTS	8
												NO BALLS					

				SCORE AT A GLANCE

BOWLER	BOWLING ANALYSIS ⊙ NO BALL + WIDE													OVS	MDS	RUNS	WKT
	1	2	3	4	5	6	7	8	9	10	11	12	13				
1 M.LEAR	·:·	11	W	·:·	✕									4	1	10	1
2 T.COLLINGE	·W·		✕											2	0	25	2
3 C.SEBASTIEN	1· ·2·	··	4·1· ··	·3· ·2·	✕									4	0	14	0
4 H.KNIGHT	2··	M	11·		✕	124								4	1	11	3
5 E.DAVIES	··2· 2·2·	4·· ···	··1· 11··											4	0	17	0
6 T.VELLACOTT	·+· 11·	13· 1·+												2	0	10	0
7																	
8																	
9																	

INNINGS OF GLORY GARDENS........ TOSS WON BY W.W... WEATHER GOOD...

BATSMAN	RUNS SCORED	HOW OUT	BOWLER	SCORE
1 J. PADGETT	4·1 >>	ct KATZ	REIFER	5
2 M. ROSE	1·1·1·1·1·1·1·1·1·1·1· >>	bowled	KATZ	12
3 A. NAZAR	2·2·1·1·4· >>	lbw	PRESTON	10
4 C SEBASTIEN	4·1·2·2·1·2 >>	lbw	KATZ	12
5 E. DAVIES	1·1·1·1·1·2·1·1 >>	ct GALE	T. WOOD	10
6 H. KNIGHT	1·1·1·4·1·1·2 >>	ct GALE	A. WOOD	12
7 F. ALLEN	1· >>	ct PRESTON	A. WOOD	1
8 T. VELLACOTT	>>	RUN	OUT	0
9 M. LEAR		NOT	OUT	0
10 P. BENNETT	1· >>	St GALE	T. WOOD	1
11				

FALL OF WICKETS

SCORE	9	24	40	47	66	67	67	69	71	10
BAT NO	1	3	4	2	5	7	8	6	10	

BYES	
L.BYES 1·1·1·1	4
WIDES 1·1·1	3
NO BALLS 1	1

TOTAL EXTRAS 8

TOTAL 71 FOR 9 WKTS

SCORE AT A GLANCE

BOWLER	BOWLING ANALYSIS ⊙ NO BALL + WIDE													OVS	MDS	RUNS	WKT
	1	2	3	4	5	6	7	8	9	10	11	12	13				
1 W. REIFER	·+4 1·1	·1W ·22	··· 14·	·14 +1·	X									4	0	23	1
2 P. PRESTON	M	·1 111	·1 w··	·221 ···	X									4	1	10	1
3 L. KATZ	2·· 1·W	··1 ·1·	·1W ··1	1·4 +1·	X									4	0	12	2
4 T. WOOD	··1 ··1	1·1 1··	1·· 1W1	w										3·1	0	8	2
5 A. WOOD	·11 1+·1	1·· 2+1·	W·2 W1⊙											3	0	14	2
6																	
7																	
8																	
9																	

Chapter Four

After the game Kiddo disappeared. I had been wondering what he was going to say about our performance and he'd just gone home as if he wasn't interested.

Liam came over to me to thank us for the game and congratulated me on my hat trick. But I wasn't in the mood for celebrating. I kept thinking everything that had gone wrong was my fault – Trevor's bowling, the catch off Liam, the field placing, getting out to a stupid shot.

There we all were sitting around in the pavilion and no one was saying much until Jo came to the rescue.

"D'you want to know what I thought of you?" she said.

"Not much," said Frankie.

She pulled out a piece of paper and showed us.

Six Good Things
1 Everyone bowled well. Especially Marty and Cal.
2 Hooker got a hat trick.
3 Five batsmen got 10 or more.
4 Matthew is a good opening bat.
5 Erica caught a brilliant catch.
6 We didn't give up.

Six Bad Things
1 The fielding was awful (except Azzie and Erica).
2 We dropped three catches – and Francis missed an easy stumping.
3 Trevor was a terrible bowler.
4 Francis batted like an idiot!
5 Their umpire was a big cheat!
6 Ohbert's shorts!!!

"Oh dear, life's not worth living any more," said Frankie, pretending to strangle himself with his wicket-keeper's gloves. He sank to the floor and gasped, "Tell them I was driven to suicide by my own sister's poisonous pen."

We ignored him – what else can you do?

"Do you really think Fingers was deliberately cheating?" asked Tylan.

"Of course he was," said Cal. "And if that's how he goes on in a friendly, imagine what he'd be like in a League game."

"Outrageous!" said Tylan. "You know, without Fingers and baby Trev, we could have won."

"Yeah, Trevor, what a creep – running off home at half-time like that," said Frankie. "Still it was worth it for the kamikaze ball. Kerrrrrpow! You ought to practise bowling that one, Cal. It's deadly."

By the time we went home, we were all feeling better about the game – all except Jason and Erica who hadn't said a word since the end of the match. Jason kept scowling at her but at least he was keeping his mouth shut.

I walked home with Cal and he told me he'd tried to have a talk with both of them. "If he keeps going on like this I don't think Erica'll play for us much longer. She's really fed up and it can't be easy for her being the only girl on the pitch."

"So what do we do? Drop Jason?"

"Don't tempt me. He didn't have a very good game, did he?" Cal grinned wickedly. "I think he's jealous of her, you know. But we can't afford to lose any players right now – what we need is at least two new ones."

"Do you think he'll ever see sense?" I asked.

"Yeah, Jason's not completely brainless. My guess is he'll come round in the end," said Cal. "We'll just have to make sure he doesn't drive Erica away before then."

By the time I got home I'd decided it hadn't been a bad start for Glory Gardens and I was even feeling strong enough to face Lizzy.

"Here comes Capt'n Hook," she said to Mum as soon as I

walked in. "Bet he lost."

"Yeah, but I got a hat trick."

"Where? Let me see."

"I'll show it to you later," I said.

"Oh go on, I want to see it now."

"I've left it tied up in the front garden," I said.

Lizzy rushed out of the house and I sat down to a late tea. I was starving.

———————•———————

Next morning at school I got a message from Kiddo. He wanted to see the whole team in his classroom at lunchtime. Jason was off sick and, of course, Matthew wasn't there because he doesn't go to our school, but the rest of us hurried along to hear what Kiddo had to say.

I still thought it was strange that he hadn't even said goodbye after the game. Frankie's theory was that he'd been driven off by the smell of Tylan's socks stinking out the changing room. "Don't worry," he said to me. "What can Kiddo say? It was a good game, we weren't thrashed – even though we only had nine players and Ohbert. And you got a hat trick."

We peered into Kiddo's room and he was sitting at his desk looking deadly serious. He told us to sit down and got up and shut the door. "Well," he said at last. "Call yourselves cricketers, do you?"

"We weren't that bad," said Cal.

"Yeah, we'd have won if it hadn't been for Trevor and F . . . I mean that umpire," said Tylan.

"I'm not talking about winning," Kiddo said, "I'm talking about playing cricket. And you can all forget about playing at the Priory if you don't learn a few basic facts – and fast."

We stared at him. What was all this stuff about facts? All right, we'd dropped a couple of catches. And the batting had collapsed at the end. Maybe he didn't like Ohbert's shorts.

"I suppose I'll have to spell it out for you," he sighed. "If

37

one more player in this team argues with the umpire or has a silly tantrum because he doesn't think he's out, then I'll wash my hands of the lot of you and you can go back and play on your Rec."

We all looked at Cal. "B . . . but that umpire didn't know the rules," he said. "Or if he did he was cheating."

"Listen," said Kiddo. "He gave Erica out and she walked. I could see from the boundary he'd got it wrong. But she didn't stand there arguing, did she?"

"I only said, 'You've got to be joking'," said Cal. "I didn't swear at him."

"I should hope not. And he wasn't joking, was he?" Kiddo sat down. "Look, right or wrong, if you don't play to the umpire's decision you might as well not turn up. Understood?"

"Yeah," said Cal quietly.

"Do you think he was trying to help them win?" asked Tylan.

"I shouldn't think so," said Kiddo. "But even if he was, when he says 'Out', it's out. Right?"

"Okay," we all said.

"Then I won't say any more," said Kiddo. "Now I suppose you want to know what I thought of your performance?"

We looked at him anxiously.

"I was really impressed," he said. "I think we've got the makings of a champion team."

"We are the champions!" chanted Frankie beginning his war dance.

"Not yet you're not," said Kiddo. "Not by a long shot. You've all got an awful lot to learn. Let's face it, you lost to a better team. But perhaps not that much better. They were more organised and they knew more about building an innings – but I think you've got every bit as much talent." He hesitated for a moment as his eyes fell on Ohbert and he coughed. Then he continued, "What you need is some coaching in the basics – things like moving your feet when you're

38

batting, watching the ball and getting your body behind it when you're fielding. And you've got to learn to play for each other – like a team."

"Okay," said Cal. "What do we do?"

"Come to net practice on Saturday morning at the Priory and I'll show you," said Kiddo.

———————— • ————————

Nets were brilliant. Everyone turned up except Tylan. We knew he was having some trouble with his dad. Tylan's old man has a stall on the Horse Fair Market and he makes Tylan work for him for nothing every Saturday. Tylan said he would try and sneak off for net practice but the escape plan hadn't worked.

Kiddo brought along two players from the Eastgate Priory Firsts and they bowled at us and gave us a lot of tips. One of them was their opening fast bowler, Dave Wing, and he showed me and Marty how to bowl an out-swinger (except it's an in-swinger for me because I bowl left-handed).

You have to keep the ball shiny on one side to help it swing through the air. Marty picked it up straight away but I found it really hard, probably because I was trying to work everything out back-to-front for the left-arm action.

Another good idea of Dave's was to mark out a target area on the wicket for the bowlers to pitch the ball in. You then count how many of your balls pitch on target. It was quite difficult. Marty got 13 out of 20; I got 11; Ohbert got none. Let's face it, Ohbert would have got none out of a hundred. Most of the balls he bowled went outside or over the top of the net and he was bowling with his Walkman on, so I'm not sure he knew what he was supposed to be doing, anyway.

Marty bowls the outswinger. He holds the ball with the seam running between his first two fingers and pointing towards the slips. He tries to bowl close to the wicket keeping his left shoulder pointing down the pitch for as long as possible in the delivery stride. As he lets go of the ball his fingers should be behind it with the wrist firm. The follow-through takes his bowling arm across his body.

We finished the session with some fielding practice. Kiddo hit the ball to us, in the air or along the ground, and we had to run in and catch it or pick up and throw to Frankie over the stumps.

After about an hour and a half, we were all getting pretty tired. Kiddo called a halt and we went back to the pavilion for a drink.

Kiddo told me he'd tried to enter us for the North County

40

Mark out the target area using anything you can get your hands on – ribbon or tape or even an old mat or a piece of a sheet. Keep records of your performance each time and you will see how your accuracy improves. (Warning: don't bowl to a batsman when you are practising like this. The ball can easily hit the edge of the mat and fly up.)

League but it was too late for this year. "I've got another idea, though," he said. "That's if you want to play some proper games."

I listened to his plan. He told me that a local business had given some money to the Club to encourage young cricketers and Kiddo's idea was to start a new, knockout cup competition for Under 11s. He said it would be called the Priory Cup.

"I reckoned that several teams from the local clubs and primary schools would be interested in playing in an Under 11s Cup," he said. "So, after I saw you lot play on Wednesday, I made a few phone calls."

I looked at him impatiently.

He picked up a cricket bat and handed it to me. "How'd you like to win that?" he asked.

The bat was signed by every cricketer in the England team.

"Let's have a look," said Frankie, rushing over and grabbing the bat. We all tried to read the signatures on its blade.

Eventually, Kiddo broke in, "I take it that means 'Yes, you're interested'. Well, you'd better have a look at this then." He unfolded a large sheet of paper and spread it out on the table in front of us.

PRIORY CUP

Group 1	*Group 2*
Birtly Parks	Lawrence Gubdale
Glory Gardens	Primary School
Our Lady of Lourdes	Mudlarks
Primary School	Orchard Pies
Stoneyheath & Stockton	Wyckham Wanderers

Week 1 Birtly Parks v Glory Gardens
Our Lady of Lourdes v Stoneyheath & Stockton
Lawrence Gubdale v Mudlarks
Orchard Pies v Wyckham Wanderers

Week 2 Birtly Parks v Our Lady of Lourdes
Glory Gardens v Stoneyheath and Stockton
Lawrence Gubdale v Orchard Pies
Mudlarks v Wyckham Wanderers

Week 3 Stoneyheath & Stockton v Birtly Parks
Our Lady of Lourdes v Glory Gardens
Wyckham Wanderers v Lawrence Gubdale
Orchard Pies v Mudlarks

Week 4 *Semi Finals*
Group 1 Winner v Group 2 Runner up
Group 2 Winner v Group 1 Runner up

Week 5 FINAL

"Who are Orchard Pies?" said Frankie, "I bet we could stuff them for breakfast."

"They're the factory on Cromwell Road," said Erica. "My aunt works there."

"Does she play cricket for them?" asked Jason.

That was quite funny for Jason and even Cal had to smile. Erica looked furious though.

The fixture list meant we had to play at least three games before the knockout stage. The first one would be a tough one according to Kiddo. Most of the best cricketers from the town's posh independent school, the Frinton, played for Birtly Parks. We called them the Partly Berks, and it suited them. But they had some good cricketers because they played at school every week. At least we weren't in the same group as Wyckham Wanderers.

Kiddo gave me a copy of the fixture list and we went off to make our plans. We had ten days to get ready for the game. The first thing was to find another player. I looked at Ohbert. No, two players. Definitely!

Chapter Five

It was Jo's idea to call a meeting of Glory Gardens Cricket Club. We met at Cal's house on Sunday afternoon because his parents and brother and sister were all out.

"I declare this first meeting of Glory Gardens C.C. open," said Jo after we had all sat down. She passed round a sheet of paper to each of us. I looked at mine; it had been done on Jo's PC, so it looked very official.

MEETING OF GLORY GARDENS C.C.
Sunday, 23rd May at Cal's House

AGENDA
1 Appointments and Elections
  Captain
  Vice Captain
  Secretary
  Treasurer
2 Club rules
3 Finding some new players
4 What shall we do about Tylan's dad?
5 How can we get some new kit?
6 Anything else to discuss?

Jo's what you call 'organised'. I sometimes can't believe she's Frankie's sister because they are so completely different. She wears serious clothes and always looks what my mum calls 'smart'; he's a clothes slob – nothing ever fits him and bits of Frankie are always sticking through the holes in his shirts and trousers. She's good at everything at school especially maths; he's hopeless – or, to be exact, hopelessly lazy. She worries; he hasn't got a care in the world. It's probably true that, without Jo, Glory Gardens C.C. wouldn't exist. And, it's a definite fact that Frankie wouldn't remember to turn up for games if Jo didn't organise him. He probably wouldn't even remember to get out of bed.

"What's all this about elections?" said Cal reading his Agenda. "We've already got a captain."

"I think Frankie should be captain," said Jason – you can guess why.

"So do I," said Frankie. "And if you elect me I'll make Ohbert vice-captain if he gives me my 50p back."

Ohbert wasn't listening. He had his Walkman on full volume.

"Don't be ridiculous, Francis," said Jo. She is the only person who calls Frankie by his proper name. "We'd be laughed out of the Cup with you as captain. Anyway you need a seconder."

After that Frankie admitted he didn't want to be captain and I was voted in – 'unanimously', according to Jo. There was a bit of fuss about who should be treasurer because Frankie said he'd do that instead if there was money in it. Jo said he couldn't be trusted with money because he was always forgetting where he put things.

"Call this a democratic meeting," said Frankie. "I propose Jo Allen for Dictator."

In the end, we had a vote between Frankie and Matthew for treasurer and Matthew won by three votes. Jo gave Frankie a little smile of victory and, for once, he looked rather upset. But being Frankie he soon bounced back.

"Can't see much point in having a treasurer anyway," he said. "We haven't got any money, have we?"

So these were the appointments that Jo wrote down in her

book which had 'Minutes of Meeting of Glory Gardens C.C.' neatly printed on the front cover.

Captain: Hooker Knight
Vice Captain: Marty Lear
Secretary: Jo Allen
Treasurer: Matthew Rose

Jo obviously had to be secretary and run the meetings because she was the only person who knew anything about it.

Cal and Marty wanted to get on with finding some new players for the team but Jo said we had to do 'Rules' next because it was next on the Agenda. So we did 'Rules'.

"It's funny how Cal goes along with everything Jo says," whispered Azzie to me and Frankie. "He normally likes to get his own way."

"I think she's got a strange power over people," said Frankie glumly. "There are rumours about her flying about at night on a broomstick."

In the end we could only agree on three rules because we didn't see the point of rules really. In fact, Glory Gardens only ever had three rules.

RULE 1   The Captain, Vice Captain and Secretary will be the selection committee and no one will argue about the teams they pick even if they are wrong.

RULE 2   Everyone will come to net practice if they can, although we know Tylan has problems with his dad's stall.

RULE 3   No one shall throw bats about in the changing room especially if it's not his/her own bat.

Then, at last, we got down to talking about new players.

"We don't want to finish up with another Trevor," said Frankie.

"That would be outrageous," said Tylan. "Never ever Trevor." Sometimes Tylan can be nearly as weird as Frankie.

"There must be someone good at school," I said. But the more we talked about it, the more we realised it wasn't going to be that easy. Most of the boys who are good at sport aren't interested in playing cricket and those who may be interested aren't any good. We decided to talk to Acfield Todd. He's a decent footballer though he doesn't have much of a clue about cricket. Still we were desperate and he would be better than Ohbert.

Then Matthew had a brilliant idea. "I think we should advertise," he said. He told us that his mum works for the Gazette and he thought she might be able to get us a free advertisement.

It took us nearly an hour to write the advert because everyone had different ideas about what to put. This was what it looked like in the end.

<u>Wanted</u> One or more brilliant cricketers (especially a fast bowler) to play for Glory Gardens Cricket Club in the Priory Cup. Apply to Hooker Knight at 20 Bason Street. Phone 241660. Urgent! (Must qualify as "Under 11")

By now we were all getting rather tired of the Meeting, so Jo suggested we should 'adjourn' and have some of the drinks and cakes that Cal's mum had provided. We discovered that Ohbert had already eaten half the cakes while we were writing the ad.

"Oh but, I didn't know they weren't for eating yet," he said, as Cal and Marty held him upside down by his feet and shook him. A cassette, an old conker, a plastic frog and a packet of chewing gum fell out of his pockets. Cal shared out the chewing gum.

"Pity, he must have spent my 50p," murmured Frankie.

We never got back to the proper Agenda but Tylan told us

all about his dad and the market stall.

"I can't get out of it. He says he can't afford to pay anyone to work with him, so I have to do it. It's not that bad because it's really busy and sometimes people tell you to keep the change. I made over two quid last week."

"What do you sell?" asked Azzie.

"Knickers."

"Knickers?"

"Knickers."

"Only knickers?" grinned Frankie.

"Mostly," said Tylan. "Sometimes we have socks and tights and swimming cozzies, too."

"Do you think you could get me a pair of boxers?" asked Ohbert.

"Oh shut up, Ohbert," said Jo. "We're supposed to be working out ways of getting Tylan away from his knickers and into Nets."

"Why don't we all take turns," said Erica. "If a different one of us works on the stall each Saturday, everyone would get a fair share of net practice. And if they earn any money it can go into club funds."

"You won't catch me selling knickers," said Jason.

"No, only wearing them," said Frankie.

Jo told them both to shut up and most of us agreed it was an excellent idea. So Tylan said he'd ask his dad.

"Who'll volunteer for next Saturday?" I asked.

"Do you think I'll get a pair of boxer shorts?" said Ohbert.

"Of course," we all said. So that was agreed.

Chapter Six

Next week was busy. I saw Acfield Todd at school and he said he'd think about playing for us – though he didn't sound too keen. On Thursday the advertisement appeared in the Gazette. They got my name wrong – it said 'Hodcer' instead of Hooker. So, when a small kid with glasses stood on our doorstep that evening and said, with a puzzled look, "Are you Hodcer?" I knew that he'd come about the advert.

His name was Jacky Gunn and he said he was a fairly quick bowler. His family had just moved into town and he was really keen to get into a cricket team. I thought he looked too small for a fast bowler but I told him to come along to Nets on Saturday anyway.

That same evening I also had two phone calls about the advert. One was Frankie putting on a silly German accent.

"Ah, Hodcer, so I am looking for ze cricket team to play for," he said. "By ze way, Hodcer, zis is a most funny name you have, ya? Vere are you coming from? Germany or Sweden? Do zay play ze cricket in Sweden?" I heard Azzie laughing in the background and told Frankie to clear off.

The other call was from someone called Clive da Costa. He said he'd come along to Nets, too.

On Saturday morning, I soon discovered I'd been wrong about Jacky. He bowled as fast as Marty and, because he was short, the ball seemed to skid off the pitch. He bowled Azzie with the second ball Azzie faced from him. That was good enough for me.

Clive da Costa didn't turn up until Nets were half over. He mumbled something about getting lost. When it came to his turn to bat it was easy to see he was something special. He was a left-hander, which was really useful, because the rest of us all bat right-handed. But it was the way he batted which made everyone sit up and take notice. He seemed to have tons of time to get into position to play his shots. He was strong and quick on his feet like Cal; but, unlike Cal, he didn't smack the ball or put all his strength into his shots. The result was the same, though. He could hit a cricket ball miles with no effort at all. It was like watching a cat; every movement was smooth and well-balanced. He made batting look so easy it wasn't fair. With Clive and Azzie batting for us we'd have a brilliant middle order.

From the start though, I could see it wasn't going to be easy with Clive. He knew he was good and he didn't mind telling everyone how good. There was an arrogance about the way he played and the way he talked. And he just didn't seem to care about upsetting people. He ignored Frankie's jokes, which, perhaps, wasn't a bad idea. But he also accused Cal of chucking when he bowled at him which, as you can imagine, didn't go down too well with Cal. He acted as if he was too good for fielding practice by larking about and then throwing the ball in to Frankie so hard that Frankie had to go and put his hands under a cold tap. That was the only time Clive laughed all morning – but I could see from the way Kiddo looked at him, that he wasn't amused.

After Nets, we had a selection meeting. It was amazing – we actually had 13 players to choose from because, on Wednesday, Acfield Todd had told Cal he'd play for us although he wasn't interested in coming along to Nets. That ruled him out of playing under Rule 2, Jo said. So in the end it came down to playing Clive or Ohbert.

"No contest," said Marty. "It's like choosing between a Ferrari and my dad's old bike."

Jo wasn't sure. "Ohbert's useless but he's been with us from the beginning. I don't think Clive will be that reliable."

Ohbert hadn't been at Nets because he was working on Tylan's dad's stall. Tylan had managed to persuade his dad that it was a good idea, but he said he wasn't sure his old man would be quite so keen after a morning with Ohbert.

So it was my casting vote. I could see Jo's point but I went with Marty.

This was the team we picked to play the Partly Berks (in batting order):

Matthew Rose
Hooker Knight (capt)
Azzie Nazar
Clive da Costa
Cal Sebastien
Erica Davies
Jason Padgett
Frankie Allen
Tylan Vellacott
Jacky Gunn
Marty Lear
Ohbert Bennett (first reserve)

Ohbert didn't seem to mind when we told him. He'd had such a good morning working with Tylan's dad and he showed us his new boxer shorts. They were red with gold stars. I felt a bit guilty when he handed over to Matthew the £4.25 he'd earned. Tylan was amazed to hear from Ohbert that they'd sold a record number of knickers. "Your dad was so pleased he wants me to work for him every Saturday – instead of you." He was even more amazed when he got home and discovered it was true.

Jason was more of a problem. He wasn't pleased about being dropped as opening bat. But to be below Erica in the batting order was the final insult.

"You could have dropped her and played Acfield and then we'd have had a proper team," he said to me.

Play it cool, I thought – no good starting another big row. So I just said, "But don't you think Erica's miles better than Acfield?"

"Don't be daft, she's a girl," said Jason.

There was no point in arguing with someone whose brain had fossilised but I couldn't resist it any longer. "Listen, Jace," I said. "There are at least five players in the side I'd drop before Erica . . . and you're one of them."

I thought I'd done it then – I was quite expecting him to tell me I could stuff Glory Gardens and he'd never play for us again. Instead he shrugged his shoulders and said, "We'll see about that. You wait till Wednesday." And he walked off.

On Wednesday morning, Azzie didn't come to school. His dad sent a note saying he was sick and wouldn't be able to play cricket either. So Ohbert was back.

———————— • ————————

The Partly Berks' ground is not far from school and most of us walked there. Kiddo gave Erica and Marty a lift because he bumped into them as he was leaving school.

I lost the toss and their captain (he said his name was Lewis Ashbeigh and he even spelt it for me) put us in.

Clive was late arriving.

"D'you get lost again?" asked Frankie, when he finally turned up.

Clive just gave him a cold look. I was a bit annoyed and I nearly moved him down the batting order but thought it best to have our top bat in number three, particularly with Azzie not playing.

It didn't make much difference. Within 10 minutes, we were 12 for four with our four best players out.

Matthew was lbw in the first over for one and then I was caught trying to play a ball down the leg side. It hit the out-side edge of my bat and lobbed back to the bowler for an easy return catch.

In the next over Clive ran out Cal going for a stupid short single. Cal wasn't pleased about it but at least he didn't throw my bat through the changing room wall because he wasn't using it. Then Clive hit a brilliant four through the covers but

The perfect cover drive from Clive with his foot to the pitch of the ball.

was caught next ball – going for a big lazy swing over square-leg which, instead, landed straight in the fielder's hands.

I told Jason to play carefully and get his eye in. But as I spoke to him I saw what I'd done. Disaster! He was going out to bat with Erica! I must have been crazy to put them next to each other in the batting order.

I could hardly bear to watch. Would they try and run each other out? Or maybe they'd just beat each other to death with their bats in the middle of the pitch.

"This could be fun," said Cal.

"Like World War Three," said Frankie.

What actually happened was stranger still. So strange that none of us could quite believe it. Right from the beginning

Erica and Jason seemed to have an understanding. They scored slowly but steadily against the opening bowlers, taking all the singles they could and running brilliantly between the wickets. Then, after the eighth over, when they'd seen off the Berks' opening attack, they began to score faster against the next two bowlers who weren't quite so accurate.

Jason hit a wild four over mid-wicket. He got it right in the middle of the bat but it was a horrible cow shot and I saw Erica walking down the wicket to have words with him.

"Oh no," I thought. "He'll never listen to her."

But amazingly he settled down and started playing sensibly again. One of his shots, an off-drive for two, was the best of

Jason plays the off-drive with his left foot to the pitch of the ball and the full face of the bat comes down through the line of the shot. He locks his wrists for the check drive.

54

the whole innings, except, perhaps, for Clive's cover drive.

By the end of the twelfth over they had put on 27 together and we were back in the game. The Berks were beginning to look bothered. I don't think they were enjoying getting a lesson on how to bat from a girl. Before the match Jason would have agreed with them – but who knew what he was thinking now!

Frankie was so excited that Kiddo had to tell him to calm down.

"Another wide from the Berks!" he cheered. "Glory, Glory, Gardens. Glory Gardens for the Cup."

"That's 40 for four – Jason's got 13," said Jo, looking up from the score-book.

"Good old Jacey," said Cal. "I knew he'd learn how to bat in a girls' team one day."

Erica was finally out playing on to a ball outside the off-stump. And, an over later, Jason went, too. He took a huge lunge at a short ball, missed and was lbw, plumb in front of his stumps. They had both scored 14.

"Well batted, Jace," Erica was the first to congratulate him when he came in.

"Yeah, well done you, too," said Jason and he even smiled.

"Is it love?" whispered Tylan to Cal.

"Yeah, I think he was getting lonely out there after Erica was out," said Cal.

There were four overs left and Frankie went a bit mad and swung at everything. He missed five in a row and then hit one over mid-wicket for three to bring up the 50. In the next over he ran poor old Tylan out for a duck – the second time in two matches. Then, a couple of balls later, he took a swing at the ball which cannoned into his pads and he charged off down the pitch. Jacky Gunn sent him back but it was too late. The close fielder on the off-side ran in, picked up the ball and beat Frankie in the chase to the stumps.

"You're getting worse," said Jo when Frankie returned from his short innings. "Trouble is, you're too fat to run."

Frankie just stroked his stomach and smiled.

Jacky and Marty stayed together to the end. We finished on 61 for eight. Erica and Jason had scored nearly half the total and the Berks bowled 10 wides. The rest of the side had scored only 18 runs altogether.

Ohbert was really disappointed that he hadn't batted. "I was in the mood to take a few more 50ps off Frankie," he said.

"Never mind, Ohbert," said Frankie. "Tell you what – this time I'll give you 50p for every catch you take and you can pay me for every one you drop."

Ohbert agreed. He was the only person in the world who believed he could catch a cricket ball. He probably even thought he looked like a cricketer. I'd asked him to wear some white or grey trousers for the game – and he had. They were white all right, but made of thin nylon and his red and gold boxer shorts shone through brilliantly. He was also wearing an old Iron Maiden tee-shirt which belonged to his brother and was five sizes too big for him and on his head sat a back-to-front, yellow baseball cap pulled down over his Walkman.

Between innings Clive told me he'd like to open the bowling.

"I've sussed out the pitch," he said, "and I can bowl out these guys. Easy."

I'd already decided to open with Jacky and me and I told him I'd think about bowling him later on. He wasn't pleased.

Things didn't start too well for me. I missed a difficult, low caught and bowled chance off the second ball and followed that with two wides. I could see Clive sniggering to himself and practising his bowling action.

Jacky Gunn bowled a good over and my next one was a bit straighter. But after four overs they'd already scored 14 and I decided it was time for Marty – although I'd wanted to keep him for the end of the innings. I brought him on at my end.

Marty was really fired up. I don't know whether it was because he saw Jacky was bowling fast or maybe he was annoyed that I hadn't opened with him, but his first ball was as quick as any I've seen him bowl. The batsman got an inside edge and Frankie got one glove on a very hard chance to his left but he couldn't hold on to it. Then, an lbw appeal was turned down by the umpire, and, finally, with the fifth ball, it was third time lucky, he bowled the Partly Berks' captain – knocking out his middle stump.

Jacky then fired in a yorker which the other opener swung at, missed and the ball landed on the toe of his front boot. He squealed with pain and jumped forward, out of his crease. Cal, fielding close in on the leg side, picked up the ball and with one movement threw down the wicket. Run out by a yard. The batsman wasn't very pleased but he limped off.

The luck seemed to be turning our way at last and Marty and Jacky were now both bowling brilliantly. Next to go was their wicket-keeper, caught by Matthew in the slips off the out-swinger Marty had been practising. He was delighted and he kept showing everyone how he'd done it.

I made up my mind to gamble on an attacking field with one fielder out and the rest close to the bat or saving singles.

Having no third-man cost us a few runs off edges through the slips, but I decided wickets mattered even more than runs now. It was no good just saving runs – we had to bowl them out. And the way Marty and Jacky were bowling, we just might do it.

Owzthat! Marty got his third wicket with an edge off bat and pad to Jason at short square-leg. He stuck out a hand and knocked the ball up and then caught it on the rebound above his head.

Everyone ran up to congratulate him – including Erica.

Jacky had bowled his four overs – none for eleven – but he'd bowled just as well as Marty and deserved at least a couple of wickets. Clive was still wheeling his arm round as a hint to me to bring him on to bowl – but I ignored him. I decided to go for a complete change and bring on Cal. That didn't please Clive.

"What's the point in donkey drops?" he said. "You want to bring on someone who can bowl."

I hadn't seen much of Clive's bowling, but what I'd seen hadn't impressed me too much. Anyway, I didn't feel like letting him have his own way all the time.

"You choose the bowlers when you're captain," I said. I was getting fed up with him knowing everything.

As it was the 'donkey drops' worked. Cal tempted their new batsman down the pitch to take a big swing at a looping off-break. He missed and was stumped easily by Frankie.

"First thing you've done right in this game," said Cal to Frankie, patting him on the back.

"I nearly had the bails off before the ball arrived," said Frankie. "If you bowl any slower you'll be able to keep wicket to your own bowling and I can go home.

Marty took his fourth wicket in his last over. Clean bowled, middle stump. He finished his spell with 4 for seven. It was the best I'd ever seen him bowl.

I told Tylan to take over at Marty's end – partly because he hadn't had much of a bat and partly to annoy Clive.

His second ball was a beauty. It pitched outside the leg stump and the batsman took a swing at it and missed because the ball turned nearly six inches. It hit his leg stump half way up.

They were 35 for seven and the next batsman decided he'd nothing to lose. After watching Tylan's first ball carefully he swung the next one way behind square for four. Another slog brought him two runs over my head at mid-on. As I picked up and threw in I thought, much more of this and we're in trouble. They now needed only 20 to win with seven overs remaining. If we didn't bowl them out we'd lose.

Cal's next over went for seven runs though he had the slogger playing and missing three times.

The fifty came up. I began to wonder if I'd made a huge mistake sticking with the two spinners and Clive kept sighing and moaning every time he passed me in the field. Then Tylan bowled a short one to the slogger; he swung again and this time he got a top edge. The ball skied to mid-wicket and, yes, the fielder was under it . . . it was Ohbert. Suddenly the catch didn't look so easy. Ohbert ran in too far, realised the ball was going over his head, stopped, stuck up a hand, slipped and landed first on his bum, then on his back. His tee-shirt ballooned out and covered his head, so you could only see the white shirt and the yellow baseball cap perched on top of it and one arm stretched high . . . holding the ball.

"Outrageous catch, Ohbert," said Tylan.

"Makes them look so easy, doesn't he?" said Cal laughing helplessly.

Frankie was rubbing his eyes. "I don't believe it! That's another 50p."

But we all knew Ohbert's catch had saved us. Two balls later Tylan got a third wicket – an easy catch to Jacky at cover-point. As Cal began his last over, they needed 9 to win; we needed one wicket.

I brought the field in as close as I could. Two came from a ball that ran down the leg side. A leg bye and then another run wide of square-leg. 57 for nine. Now they only needed 5 to beat us.

"I'll try a quicker one," said Cal to me, making a secret sign to Frankie. Frankie dropped back a bit as Cal came in.

The batsman was taken completely by surprise. The ball nipped off the pitch and he jammed down his bat. Too late. It was through him. And over went the off-stump. Frankie tore off his gloves and threw them in the air with a great cry of victory.

WE'D WON.

HOME TEAM	BIRTLY PARKS	v	GLORY GARDENS	AWAY TEAM	AT BIRTLY PARKS

HOME TEAM: BIRTLY PARKS v GLORY GARDENS AWAY TEAM
AT BIRTLY PARKS   DATE JUNE 2ND

INNINGS OF...GLORY GARDENS...   TOSS WON BY B.P....WEATHER Cloudy

BATSMAN	RUNS SCORED	HOW OUT	BOWLER	SCORE
1 M. ROSE	1·	lbw	McKENZIE	1
2 H. KNIGHT	1·1·	c & b	McKENZIE	2
3 C. DA COSTA	1·1·4	ct WILDE	ASHBEIGH	6
4 C. SEBASTIEN		RUN	OUT	0
5 E. DAVIES	1·1·1·2·1·1·1·1·1·2·1	bowled	WORTHINGTON	14
6 J. PADGETT	1·1·2·1·1·4·2·1·1	lbw	COWDRAY	14
7 F. ALLEN	3·	RUN	OUT	3
8 T. VELLACOTT		RUN	OUT	0
9 J. GUNN	1·1·	NOT	OUT	2
10 M. LEAR	1·1·1·1·	NOT	OUT	4
11				

FALL OF WICKETS

	1	2	3	4	5	6	7	8	9	10
SCORE	2	5	7	12	48	48	52	53		
BAT NO	1	2	4	3	5	6	8	7		

BYES	1·	1
L.BYES	1·1·1·	4
WIDES	1·+·+·1·1·1·1·1·1·	10
NO BALLS		

TOTAL EXTRAS	15
TOTAL FOR WKTS	61 / 8

SCORE AT A GLANCE

BOWLING ANALYSIS ⊙ NO BALL + WIDE

BOWLER	1	2	3	4	5	6	7	8	9	10	11	12	13	OVS	MDS	RUNS	WKT
1 A. McKENZIE	··1 / ··W·	·W· / ·1·1	··· / ··2	X										4	0	7	2
2 L. ASHBEIGH	1·1 / ··1	··· / +·+·+·1·1	·1· / ··1	X										4	0	12	1
3 B. WORTHINGTON	·1· / 2·11	·+·+ / 141·1	·+ / ·W·	X										4	0	11	1
4 A. COWDRAY	··· / 1·4·2	··1 / 21·1	·+· / +··	X										4	0	14	1
5 N. MAXWELL	··3 / ··1·													2	0	5	0
6 B. BINLEY	·+ / ··1·	·1+ / ·111												2	0	7	0
7																	
8																	
9																	

HOME TEAM: BIRTLY PARKS **V** GLORY GARDENS (AWAY TEAM)

AT BIRTLY PARKS **DATE** JUNE 2ND

INNINGS OF BIRTLY PARKS **TOSS WON BY** B.P. **WEATHER** CLOUDY

BATSMAN	RUNS SCORED	HOW OUT	BOWLER	SCORE
1 L. ASHBEIGH	1.1.1.2.1.2.1	bowled	LEAR	9
2 J. DEVEREAUX	1.1.1.1	Run	OUT	4
3 N. MAXWELL	1.2.1.1	bowled	LEAR	5
4 W. GRABHAM-SMITH	1.1	ct ROSE	LEAR	2
5 B. BINLEY		ct PADGETT	LEAR	0
6 A. COWDRAY		st ALLEN	SEBASTIEN	0
7 O. WILDE	1.1.1	ct GUNN	VELLACOTT	3
8 B. WORTHINGTON	2.1	bowled	VELLACOTT	3
9 N. DICKMAN	4.2.1.2.2.3.2	ct BENNETT	VELLACOTT	16
10 A. McKENZIE	1.	bowled	SEBASTIEN	1
11 P. PERCY	1.2.1	NOT	OUT	4

| | | BYES | 1.1. | 2 | TOTAL EXTRAS | 10 |

FALL OF WICKETS

	1	2	3	4	5	6	7	8	9	10			
SCORE	14	16	19	25	28	30	35	51	52	57	L BYES	1.1.1.1	5
BAT NO	1	2	4	5	6	3	8	9	7	10	WIDES	1.1.1	3
											NO BALLS		

TOTAL FOR WKTS: 57 for 10

SCORE AT A GLANCE

0		70	1 2 3 4 5 6 7 8 9	140	1 2 3 4 5 6 7 8 9	210	1 2 3 4 5 6 7 8 9			
10		80	1 2 3 4 5 6 7 8 9	150	1 2 3 4 5 6 7 8 9	220	1 2 3 4 5 6 7 8 9			
20		90	1 2 3 4 5 6 7 8 9	160	1 2 3 4 5 6 7 8 9	230	1 2 3 4 5 6 7 8 9			
30		100	1 2 3 4 5 6 7 8 9	170	1 2 3 4 5 6 7 8 9	240	1 2 3 4 5 6 7 8 9			
40		110	1 2 3 4 5 6 7 8 9	180	1 2 3 4 5 6 7 8 9	250	1 2 3 4 5 6 7 8 9			
50		120	1 2 3 4 5 6 7 8 9	190	1 2 3 4 5 6 7 8 9	260	1 2 3 4 5 6 7 8 9			
60	1 2 3 4 5 6 7 8 9	130	1 2 3 4 5 6 7 8 9	200	1 2 3 4 5 6 7 8 9	270	1 2 3 4 5 6 7 8 9			

BOWLING ANALYSIS ⊙ NO BALL + WIDE

BOWLER	1	2	3	4	5	6	7	8	9	10	11	12	13	OVS	MDS	RUNS	WKT
1 H. KNIGHT	..+ .·2	..1 .1	X											2	0	7	0
2 J. GUNN	.·. .·.	1	.1. ..2	..2 ... 1	X									4	0	11	0
3 M. LEAR	W	.. .1. 1w.	.1. 1w.	.1. W.2	X									4	1	7	4
4 C. SEBASTIEN	... W.1	..1 +1.	.22 ..3	2.1 W										3.4	0	14	2
5 T. VELLACOTT	.W. 421	2W1 W.1												2	0	11	3
6																	
7																	
8																	
9																	

Chapter Seven

Wednesday, 2nd June
Priory Cup Results

Stoneyheath & Stockton *beat* Our Lady of Lourdes by 6
  wickets
Glory Gardens *beat* Birtly Parks by 4 runs
Mudlarks *beat* Lawrence Gubdale by 9 wickets
Wyckham Wanderers *beat* Orchard Pies by 24 runs

Group 1		Group 2	
Glory Gardens	4	Mudlarks	4
Stoneyheath & S'ton	4	Wyckham Wndrs	4
Birtly Parks	0	Lawrence Gub.	0
Lady of Lourdes	0	Orchard Pies	0

On Sunday night Cal and I were talking about the result and
working out the group league tables and our chances of getting through to the semis. You got four points for a win and
two for a tie or if the game was rained off.

"If we can win one more game we'll almost definitely be
through," I said.

"What's the next game?" asked Cal.

"Stoneyheath, then Lady of Lourdes."

"Are they a girls' team?" Cal asked.

"Who? Lady of Lourdes? Don't be daft, that's only the
name of the school. I think it's Catholic."

"You mean nuns and things?" said Cal. "Shouldn't think they're too brilliant at cricket then."

"Kiddo says there's no easy side in the Cup," I said. "And anyway, we've got Stoneyheath next and they're one of the favourites."

"Yeah, looks as though they beat the nuns pretty easily," said Cal. "But we'll have Azzie back for the next game, that'll make our batting a lot stronger."

"It didn't look very strong on Wednesday," I said.

"Well, it wasn't helped by Clive the Magnificent running me out, was it?"

"What do you think about Clive?" I asked. "I mean do you reckon he's going to fit in?"

Clive hadn't turned up for Nets on Saturday but we'd still picked him for the Stoneyheath game. Jo wanted to drop him but Marty persuaded me that we needed to pick our best side to stand a chance. Jo had got quite cross. "What's the point of having rules," she said, "when the first time someone breaks them you let them off." In the end though, she accepted that she was outvoted and we agreed it would be the last time Clive was allowed to get away with it.

With Azzie back that meant we'd dropped Ohbert again. Ohbert hadn't been at Nets either – he was working on Tylan's old man's knicker stall once more. It was really Erica's turn but Ohbert had offered to take her place and Erica didn't need asking twice. This time Ohbert handed over £7.50 to Matthew for club funds but I've got to say he didn't seem quite so 'unbothered' about not being picked for the game.

"Oh but . . . it's not because I didn't come to Nets, is it?" he'd asked me.

I told him that it wasn't the reason. 'Rule No. 2' didn't apply when you were doing the knicker stall and anyway Ohbert was earning a fortune for us – we'd soon have enough to buy a club bat. There wasn't much point in him practising anyway.

I felt bad about dropping Ohbert, particularly as everyone

was talking about his catch. And that wasn't all they were talking about.

"Frankie and Jacky Gunn are really dead against having Clive in the team," said Cal. "And I don't think Matt's very keen either, except he doesn't say much."

"At least that means Frankie and Jo are agreed on something," I said. "But what do you think?"

"Well, he's a good cricketer all right – brilliant, in fact. But he's a terrible big head. Thinks he's better than all of us put together. You should have heard what he said about your captaining."

"That I should have opened the bowling with him, I suppose?"

"Yes, and your field placing was terrible and you don't know a thing about which end to bowl your bowlers from which isn't surprising because you can't bowl yourself and what he'd do is . . . "

"Wait a minute, we won, didn't we?" I said. "And no thanks to Clive."

"Yeah. Take no notice," said Cal. "Clive's a bit screwed up – mind you it's not surprising if what my mum tells me is true."

Cal told me his mum had known the da Costa family years ago. She'd worked with Clive's mother and met his dad and Clive at work once or twice. They'd seemed a very happy family. Then Mrs da Costa was knocked down by a hit-and-run driver and died in hospital weeks later. Clive's dad was completely destroyed by it. He started drinking a lot and things went downhill fast. Eventually he lost his job and got hopelessly into debt.

"Mum hasn't seen him since we moved," said Cal. "They got slung out of their house and she thinks Clive's now living with his old man on the Lillee Estate. She reckons Clive sort of looks after himself and his dad virtually lives in the pub."

"Wow. Not surprising Clive's a bit weird then," I said.

"Yeah, makes you think," said Cal. He smiled. "But that

doesn't help Glory Gardens, does it? Which reminds me, in case you were wondering, *I* thought you captained pretty well."

I remembered what Kiddo had said to me on Saturday. That I'd done well but that it's easy to captain a winning side. It's when you're losing that it gets really tough, particularly when you're losing badly. I thought back to the Wyckham game when I'd nearly decided to pack it in.

Glory Gardens wasn't turning out to be an easy team to captain, either. First there was Trevor, then Erica and Jason and now Clive. I sometimes thought we needed a psychiatrist more than a captain. I was half expecting a revolution to break out at the game on Wednesday evening – but I'd just have to wait and see.

In the end nothing happened on Wednesday. The Stoneyheath Club secretary rang Kiddo on Monday and asked if we could put off the game till Friday evening. Their first team had a rearranged league match and they couldn't find anyone to bring the junior team to the Priory ground. It wasn't a problem for any of us, so Kiddo agreed.

———— ● ————

On Thursday at school, Kiddo told me the other Wednesday evening results. Birtly Parks had beaten Lady of Lourdes easily, by seven wickets. And both Wyckham and Orchard Pies had won their games in Group Two.

"Your next game's a tough one, kiddo," he said. "If you want to know what I think then peg back your ears."

Oh no, lecture time, I thought. But I had to admit that Kiddo knew a lot about cricket so I tried to concentrate on what he was saying. Most of it was pretty obvious stuff – "try and keep it tight", "no throwing away your wickets playing fancy shots", "if it hadn't been for Erica and Jason, you'd have lost last week" and so on.

Then he said, "I've just had a thought about your batting order. Have you considered opening with young Calvin?"

I hadn't – and nor had Cal.

"Well, first of all, kiddo," said Kiddo, "you'd be more use down the order, say number five or six, where you can hold things up if there's a collapse like last week. Jason Padgett played well enough but he doesn't really like the quick stuff so he shouldn't open. Asif and that Clive are your three and four. So that leaves Erica and Calvin. Either of them could do it but I've a hunch young Calvin might make a very useful partner for Matthew Rose. He's a bit impetuous but opening might calm him down and he knows how to play straight."

Perhaps he had a point. I spent ages working out a new batting order and this is what I finally decided.

Matthew Rose	Jason Padgett
Cal Sebastien	Tylan Vellacott
Azzie Nazar	Frankie Allen
Clive da Costa	Marty Lear
Erica Davies	Jacky Gunn
Hooker Knight	

My two worries were that Jason, after batting so well, wouldn't be too pleased about going even further down the order to number seven – two places below Erica! And I wasn't sure about playing Tylan above Frankie after he'd got two ducks. Still one of them hadn't been his fault and he deserved another chance.

On Friday, the weather was awful. It rained hard in the morning and it was very windy when we went out to bat. I lost the toss as usual and they put us in. I'd have done the same. The light wasn't good and the wicket was damp enough for the bowlers to get some life out of it. I'd called tails every time so far and I was beginning to think they were using a double-headed coin.

"Oh, look at this, demoted to number nine," sighed Frankie looking at the scoresheet.

"The way you've played you should be twelfth," said Jo.

"Wait a minute, I scored three more than Cal and he's opening," said Frankie.

"If you opened the batting," said Tylan "you'd have a good chance of running out the whole team."

Frankie laughed.

Before Matthew and Cal went out I told Cal to take it easy to begin with and get his eye in. There was no need to say anything to Matthew. Clive arrived five minutes after the game had started. Azzie and Erica were already padded up and I told him he'd been moved down to five because he was late. He shrugged and said nothing.

After six overs, I was beginning to wonder if I hadn't said too much about batting straight and sensibly. We'd scored only eleven and even the singles were starting to dry up. If anything, Cal was playing more defensively than Matt.

Frankie was getting really frustrated. "What have you done to Cal?" he asked me. "He used to play like Ian Botham and you've turned him into a Geoffrey Boycott."

Each time Cal played a defensive stroke, Frankie groaned. Finally, he exploded, "Oi, Calvin!"

Cal foolishly looked up.

"It's not a five day Test Match, mate," he yelled. "Beat the ball, man." We all knew what was coming next. Frankie's favourite calypso. It goes like this:

> "Beat the ball, donkey, beat the ball,
> Cover drive going to make them fall.
> Hit it, man, like Kallicharran,
> Hit it, right in the stand."

Ohbert joined in, too. It was difficult to look at Ohbert without feeling sick – he was wearing an orange and purple striped shirt with silver sleeves and slimy green bermuda shorts. Then Azzie's dad, in spite of Azzie's protests, started to sing along, as well. He told us Kallicharran was one of the best cricketers ever to play for the West Indies. Frankie didn't care who he was; he just kept singing his song over and over again until Marty and Tylan jumped on him.

The Stoneyheath bowling was very accurate and the fielders were swooping in like vultures. It was getting dark, too, and the conditions were definitely not easy for batting. However, Frankie's calypso seemed to do the trick. Both batsmen began to open up. The second pair of bowlers weren't quite so good and they cashed in on some short stuff. Cal played a lovely pull for four and then edged a streaky three through the slips. Matt got three for a push into the covers because the extra-cover fielder was too keen and threw the ball straight over the keeper's head. There was no-one backing up and it went for two overthrows.

In the twelfth over, Cal was caught behind; but by then we were going at better than three an over. 39 for one.

Azzie came in and batted like a star for three overs. He got nearly all the bowling but, even so, 20 off 14 balls was brilliant. And he didn't even appear to be trying to score fast. He just placed the ball in the gaps and ran quickly between the wickets, getting twos where most of us would just have run a single. To be fair, Matt supported him superbly, giving Azzie most of the strike.

In the end it took a great catch at point to get him out. He edged a cover drive and it went in the air, hard and fast. The fielder dived to his left and somehow got both hands to it.

By now it was getting very dark and extremely difficult for batting. Erica was out second ball – clean bowled. Even Clive played and missed the first two balls he received. Then he hit two beautiful fours: a drive between mid-off and extra cover and a powerful pull through mid-wicket.

We were 75 for three when the rain came down. After ten minutes the pitch looked like a lake and it was obvious that cricket was over for the evening.

Kiddo explained that, under the Cup rules, both sides

Azzie plays this superb square cut with his weight completely on the back foot. Notice how his right hand is controlling the stroke and how he rolls his wrists to keep the ball down.

would get two points if the game was rained off. Before we went home, Jo worked out how the group tables stood after two games.

Group 1		*Group 2*	
Glory Gardens	6	Wyckham Wndrs	8
Stoneyheath & S'ton	6	Orchard Pies	4
Birtly Parks	4	Mudlarks	4
Lady of Lourdes	0	Lawrence Gub.	0

Clive said if it hadn't been for the weather nothing would have stopped him from scoring a supreme 50. He showed us all the shots he would have played getting there which really cheered everyone up a lot.

But Frankie looked on the bright side as usual.

"All we've got to do now is beat the Ladies," he said, "and we're through to the semifinal."

"Yeah, they must be useless," said Jason. We were all expecting him to make some embarrassing joke about girls and cricket. But, surprise, surprise, all he said was, "Even the Berks beat them easily, didn't they?"

Cal winked at me and grinned.

Chapter Eight

The next morning was Saturday. It was sunny and warm, which made last night's rain even more annoying.

When I came down to breakfast I found Lizzie picking all the best bits out of the muesli. "Mmsorryoo dinnplay lassnigh," she said through a mouthful of dried banana and raisins. I think she was trying to be friendly which was a bit of a shock so early in the morning.

Then she said, "Oh by the way, can you lend me your bike today? Mine's got a broken chain." That was more like it.

I pretended for a bit that I needed it myself but in the end I let her have it in return for a written and signed promise that if she broke anything she'd pay for it *and* that she owed me a special favour anytime I asked.

I got out of the house just as I heard Dad saying it was my turn to do the breakfast washing up.

When I arrived at Nets, Ohbert was batting! And Cal and Tylan were bowling at him.

"We decided he needed some extra practice," said Tylan.

"He hasn't hit one yet," said Cal. And he bowled a looping off-break at Ohbert which hit the middle and off-stumps while Ohbert was still groping miles outside the line.

Frankie was doing the knicker stall this Saturday. It was his turn and Ohbert had turned down the chance to do a third week because he said he needed a Net. Even Frankie couldn't argue with that. I was surprised though, because I knew how much Ohbert enjoyed working on the market. I also noticed he was batting without his Walkman for the first time and, in an Ohbertish sort of way, really trying to concentrate.

Azzie padded up in the other net and in between balls he tried to show Ohbert how to play a forward defensive shot. His first few goes weren't very successful to say the least.

At last Ohbert hit one and a great beam of a smile spread across his face. He seemed to get more pleasure from that single shot than Alec Stewart does scoring a Test Match century.

The thing to remember about playing the forward defensive is never commit yourself to the shot too early before you've picked up the length of the ball. Azzie controls the shot with a firm grip of the top hand and high front elbow.

It was a good practice session. Kiddo brought a video camera with him and filmed some of us batting. Ohbert put on the pads again at the end of practice and asked him to video his forward defensive shot. The trouble is that he's now playing forward defensive to everything, even really short balls which whistle past his ears.

Afterwards in the pavilion, Kiddo played back the video on the Club's machine. It was interesting to see the little things you do wrong without thinking. I noticed, when I was playing on the back foot, my shoulder came round and I finished up very square to the bowler. You could see it clearly

For the backward defensive shot the back foot is parallel to the crease and takes all your weight. Your eyes should be lined up with the ball, behind the handle of the bat. Look at the left elbow – held high as in the forward defensive.

when it was played back in slow motion. Kiddo said that was probably why I got caught off an outside edge against the Partly Berks. He told me to keep my back foot parallel to the crease and to practise the stroke at home in front of a long mirror.

The only bad thing about the morning was that Clive didn't show up again.

"That's it," said Jo. "We've got to drop him."

"But he might have a good excuse," said Marty.

"Then he could have rung someone," Jo insisted.

"Well, I don't think Clive needs to practise. He's the best player we've got and Ohbert's the worst. It's crazy to leave him out," said Marty.

They both looked at me. All sorts of thoughts went through my mind – Clive at home all on his own – maybe he had tried to ring me and perhaps he hadn't understood the Nets rule. But most of all I saw Ohbert's forward defensive shot. It didn't matter though, I knew what my choice had to be.

"Sorry, Mart," I said. "I'm with Jo this time. He may be the best but he's playing in a team not just for himself."

We agreed that someone had to phone Clive and tell him he'd been dropped. Jo and Marty looked at me again and I got the message. Another nice job for the captain.

When we told Ohbert he was back in the side, he grinned and said, "Oh but, er that's really great." I think he was pleased but you're never quite sure with Ohbert.

No one was sorry about Clive being dropped. Jacky was really pleased, "Good riddance," he said.

Frankie arrived at the ground while we were watching the video again. He said Ohbert's forward defensive reminded him of his goldfish at feeding time. "It's exactly the way it darts forward with its mouth open and those great bulging eyes," he said.

Frankie had earned three pounds on the stall; not as good as Ohbert but Matt said we had £14.75 now in the club fund plus another fiver which Azzie's dad had contributed because he's mad about cricket. That made nearly twenty quid.

"A decent bat will cost nearly thirty pounds," said Erica.

"It'll take us at least three weeks to earn another tenner," said Marty. "And the Cup will be over by then."

Kiddo was listening to us. "What if I lend you ten pounds, kiddoes?"

"Yeah. We could pay you back every Saturday from the knicker money," said Frankie.

"I might even let you keep it if you win the Cup for us," said Kiddo, handing Matt a ten pound note.

———— • ————

Cal, Marty, Matt and I agreed to meet after lunch at Ollie's sport's shop in Baxter Street. Ollie used to play football. He was left back for the Town but he's too fat now even to do his boots up. He's okay, though, and he often gives us old tennis balls and quite good stuff he wants to get rid of.

The cheapest bat was £25.95, but the one we all liked best was the Megapower Superbest which was £28.50. It was just the right size for Cal, but not too long or heavy for any of us.

We had enough for the bat, but I wanted to get a white shirt for Ohbert. (Actually, it was Jo's idea. "After all," she'd said, "he's earned most of the money.") The cheapest one Ollie had cost £5.95 because it was a bit shop soiled. When we told him we didn't have enough, he gave us the Megapower bat, the shirt and threw in a pair of white socks, all for £29.75. Matt counted out the money and we left before he could change his mind.

"We'd better give the socks to Tylan," said Cal. "Then we can burn his."

Marty sniffed. "That won't make any difference. Tylan's feet will soon get to work on these, you'll see."

We took the bat to my house to put some linseed oil on it.

Cal demonstrates how to choose the right bat and the classic stance. You should be able to stand comfortably with the toe of the bat resting close to your back foot. When you lift the bat it shouldn't feel too heavy. The thing about the grip is to keep both hands together with the 'Vs' formed by the thumbs in line. The stance should be comfortable with the weight evenly distributed on both feet. The classic position is to have left shoulder and head facing straight down the pitch. But a lot of batsmen prefer to be more 'square on' and some, like Graham Gooch, stand with their bat raised in the air.

Ollie had told us it should be oiled lightly and, when it had dried off a bit, we should bounce an old leather ball on the hitting area at least 1,000 times. We found some linseed oil in the garden shed and spent the rest of the afternoon working on the bat. Unfortunately, Cal spilt most of the oil on the paper bag containing Ohbert's shirt and Tylan's socks. So we had to wash them.

"Better use boiling water to get the oil out," said Marty. So I boiled up a kettle and we soaked the shirt and socks in hot water and washing-up liquid because we couldn't find any washing powder.

In the evening, after Marty and Matt had gone home, I told Cal that I had to ring Clive.

A man answered the phone, "Yeah!" He sounded very cross and I assumed it was Clive's dad.

"Can I speak to Clive, please?"

"What d'you want him for?"

"Well, it's sort of about cricket."

"Cricket, that's all that ridiculous boy ever thinks about," mumbled the voice on the phone. Then he bellowed "Clive! Come here! Someone about your damned cricket."

Clive came to the phone and before I could say anything he said, "Couldn't make Nets, right. Too busy. So, where's the game on Wednesday?"

I tried feebly to explain that it was the decision of the selection committee and he knew the rule about Nets.

There was a long silence. "So who's playing instead of me?"

"Er . . . Ohbert is."

Clive laughed. "Well, I don't want to play for a joke side anyway. So you can stuff your Glory Gardens. You'll never get anywhere without me. You'll see." And he slammed the phone down.

"He sounded pleased to hear from you," said Cal.

"If that was his dad, he's horrible," I said.

"But I was thinking about Ohbert – I couldn't get the video of his batting out of my mind. Clive's probably right, I

77

thought, and I told Cal what he had said.

"Even if he comes back grovelling, I wouldn't have him," said Cal. "Mr Swanky Clive'll get a big shock when we win the Cup. We don't need his mouth in Glory Gardens."

No, I thought, but we could do with his batting. And maybe he can't help being difficult. Certainly having a dad like that didn't help.

Then my sister came in from the garden holding out Ohbert's shirt in front of her. "What's this for? A dolly?" she asked with a giggle. So maybe the shirt had shrunk a bit.

———————— • ————————

If we'd thought that was the end of the story with Clive we were mistaken. When we came out of school on Monday, guess who was leaning up against a car opposite the school gates, staring straight at us.

Frankie, Azzie and Cal were with me and, as usual, Frankie was the first to shoot his mouth off. "Hi Clive! You're really badly lost today – wrong school!"

It was the same old silly joke – Frankie could be very irritating when he tried, or even without trying – but Clive overreacted.

"I didn't come to talk to you, blubberguts. So get lost yourself."

"Sorry, I forgot you were an international cricket star," said Frankie. "Just a pity no one wants to play with you, isn't it?"

Clive had had enough. He pushed Frankie viciously in the chest and caught him off balance. Frankie fell over backwards and – thump – landed hard in the gutter on his bum. With a cold look at me, Clive turned and walked away very slowly. Cal made a move to go for him but I stuck my arm out to stop him and put my other hand on his shoulder and he relaxed.

"No sense of humour, that kid," said Frankie smiling up from the gutter.

We'd probably never know what was on Clive's mind or why he'd come to see me. If only Frankie could learn to keep his mouth shut sometimes. Still . . . we were probably better off without Clive.

Chapter Nine

"Heads," I called.

Heads it was. I'd won my first toss. I was keen to put them in so that we could chase the runs but Azzie and Cal both told me they wanted some batting practice for the semis so I decided to bat.

I had to agree with Frankie and Tylan that 'the Ladies', as they called Our Lady of Lourdes Primary School, didn't look much like cricketers. If anything they were scruffier than Glory Gardens – none of them were in proper cricket stuff and most of them were wearing jeans.

"Their wicket-keeper can only just see over the stumps," said Frankie.

"Outrageous!" said Tylan. "I hope Cal doesn't step on him by mistake."

Even Azzie joined in; it was probably the first team we'd played against where nearly everyone was smaller than him. "It's a good thing they've cut the grass short," he said, "or we wouldn't be able to see them."

"I suppose that's why they play on a miniature pitch," said Marty.

The ground *was* very tiny. The boundary on one side was so close that cover-point was fielding right on the line. And when Marty bowled, the slips would be nearly on the boundary. I'd noticed, when I went out to toss, that the pitch was pretty rough, too. There were great big clumps of dandelions here and there in the outfield and the strip was all sorts of colours from brown to light green with one or two daisies poking through on a length at the far end.

"50p for the first six," shouted Frankie, as the game began.

Matt, as usual, watched the opening over very carefully. It was medium slow, straight but not very special. At the other end, they opened with a spin bowler. He was the slowest bowler I'd ever seen and he gave the ball so much air it almost went into orbit.

Cal stood and watched his first ball pass by with a broad grin. It was well outside the off-stump, almost a wide. I think it was the first time Cal had seen anyone bowling slower than he did. The second ball was closer to the off-stump. Cal took a huge swing aiming somewhere over extra cover, missed and was bowled off-stump. He stood and looked in disbelief for a moment and then slowly walked off.

"Quack, quack!" said Frankie as Cal passed us. "Another duck for Calvin." Frankie didn't believe in cheering people up when they were down.

Azzie faced two looping off-breaks which he played back to the bowler. Then he got a slow full toss which he swung away in the air, straight into the hands of mid-wicket.

Matt was out in the next over, to a horrible shooter – bowled middle stump.

I couldn't believe it. We were 0 for three. Not a single run on the board – and the bowling was rubbish. Well, perhaps the spinner was turning it a bit, but we should have been thrashing him all over the ground. Maybe it was the pitch?

Could Erica and Jason rescue us again? No, that was too much to hope for.

They'd put on five runs – four singles and a leg-bye – when Jason played back to a well-pitched-up ball from the spinner. It turned and kept low and he was right in front of the stumps when the ball hit his pads. "Owzat!" screamed the little off-break bowler. "Out," said Sid raising his finger.

5 for four and I was in. We'd only been playing for a quarter of an hour.

"What do we do now?" asked Erica, as I came to the wicket.

I realised I hadn't got a plan. We were in a big mess and I wasn't sure whether to tighten things up or hit our way out of trouble.

"Don't take any chances and push the quick singles," I said.

I tried to do just that. But it wasn't easy against the spinner. He was bowling so slowly that there was no pace on the ball. If you just pushed at it, it went nowhere. His fielders were all in saving singles and it was difficult to get the ball through without giving it a real smack. I kept looking at that tempting leg side boundary. Then a big looping ball arrived slightly down the leg side. I swung at it and connected. The ball bounced just inside the boundary in front of square. Four runs. That was better. The next ball was a bit straighter but I played the same shot and missed. Click. I heard that horrible noise and knew when I turned round I'd see the bails lying on the ground.

I looked at Erica in despair. She shrugged. I couldn't blame her for being annoyed. I'd completely ignored my own instructions to her. One wild shot and we were now 13 for five.

"Come on, Our Lady of Lourdes! Come on, Our Lady of Lourdes!" chanted the home supporters.

On a better day, Frankie would have thought that was pretty funny. But even he had nothing to say now. There was a glum silence hanging over the Glory Gardens team when I walked back to join them.

"Hard luck, Hooker," mumbled Cal, at last.

"Stupid shot," I said. Now we were down to Tylan, Frankie, Marty and Jacky. Could one of them pull the innings round?

Tylan's luck was still out. He got his bat tangled up in his pads as he was running a quick single and fell over. Before he could get up he was run out. Another duck.

Frankie decided it was death or glory. He took a huge, horrible swing at a well-pitched-up ball and turned it into a yorker. The ball bounced under his bat and hit his off-stump. How could I criticise him, though? I'd done just the same.

Marty edged a single and then pushed at one of the slow loopers and the ball dollied up to the close fielder at silly mid-off.

That was the end of the little off-break bowler. He'd finished his four overs. And he'd destroyed us. Or maybe we'd destroyed ourselves by the way we'd played him. Still, there were his figures for all to see.

	Overs	Mdns	Runs	Wkts
M. Calverley	4	1	7	5

At 16 for eight there was really no way back for us. All the fielders were crowding the bat and it looked as if it were just a matter of time. Thanks to a leg bye, Erica kept Jacky away from the bowling for a couple of overs but he was eventually out stumped as he stretched forward out of his crease. He was the sixth Glory Gardens player to get a duck. Would Ohbert make it seven? More than likely.

Ohbert walked out to the wicket all in white except for his red baseball cap. He had managed to squeeze into his new shirt but it was so tight he could hardly breathe and, although he kept pulling it down, there was a strip of Ohbert showing between it and the top of his trousers.

The first ball he received was short; he played an immaculate forward defensive and the ball bounced off his baseball cap. Ohbert rubbed his head thoughtfully and waited for the next delivery.

This time the ball snicked the outside edge of his forward lunge and first slip dropped it. Erica called a single. It was the last ball of the over, so Ohbert had unfortunately kept the bowling. But Erica was right to take the single, we needed every run we could get.

Frankie groaned. He had a new bet with Ohbert: 50p for every run he scored more than Frankie. Ohbert was already

50p up because Frankie had got a duck.

Mind you, it didn't look as if Ohbert was going to add to that. He played four more classical forward defensives – the bat never got within a foot of the ball which in turn went over middle stump, shaved the off-stump, bounced off his bum and hit him on the shoulder. The Ladies were throwing up their hands, sighing, appealing – but Ohbert was still there. Then, Ohbert got a straight well-pitched-up ball on middle stump. It called out for a forward defensive stroke. But, for some reason, this time Ohbert decided to play his other shot – the old cross back swing. We all winced. He got a bottom edge to the ball and it bounced sharply in front of the stumps and rebounded over the top of them, over the little wicket-keeper's head and landed on a pullover that one of the slips had taken off and left behind the keeper. Sid walked over to the square-leg umpire and after a brief word with him signalled five runs.

He told us afterwards that it's a rule that if the ball hits anything the fielders have put on the ground, five runs are awarded to the batting side. Since Ohbert hit it, it was five to him.

Frankie couldn't believe it. "That's three quid," he moaned.

"Outrageous," shouted Tylan. "Come on, Ohbert. Make it a tenner."

Ohbert grinned at us, took another wild swing at the next ball, somehow half connected again and charged off down the wicket for a run. Erica screamed at him to go back. The ball had gone straight to silly mid-on who threw to the keeper. Ohbert turned, slipped and fell on his nose. On his hands and knees he watched the keeper take off the bails.

We were all out for 23. And Ohbert was top scorer with 6. That said it all.

Erica walked slowly towards us; she wasn't pleased. "You were all pathetic," she said.

No one argued. It was true. Apart from Matt, every one of us had thrown our wicket away and we knew we'd probably wrecked our chances of going through to the semifinals. The

Ladies had bowled us out in twelve overs which meant we'd wasted eight. The golden rule in limited overs cricket is to make sure you bat out all your overs.

"We'll just have to bowl them out for 22," said Frankie.

"Not much chance of that," said Marty gloomily.

It was a more serious and determined Glory Gardens that took to the field just after 6 o'clock. I thought of bowling Cal from the beginning to see if a spinner could work the magic twice. But in the end I opened with Marty and Jacky. Marty was trying too hard to bowl really fast and he gave away three wides. But Jacky was on target as usual and he had a wicket in his first over, clean bowled. It would have been two if Matt had held on to a difficult chance at second slip.

I decided to take Marty off after two overs and bring on Cal. By that time they were 11 for one – nearly half-way there – and Jim Hunt, their little keeper who had opened the batting, was showing us how to play on a difficult track. He got behind everything and played forward whenever he could. But when Marty bowled him a loose long hop, he pulled it strongly to the short leg side boundary.

Cal bowled beautifully. He took a sharp caught and bowled chance in his first over. In his second, he had two wickets in two balls – a good catch at backward short-leg by Jason and an even better one by Azzie in the slips. Jacky was given an lbw in his last over – I think he got it for the loudest appeal I've ever heard, because we all thought the ball was going down the leg side. Still, it was their umpire who gave it.

They were now 17 for five. Only 7 runs needed – we were in with a chance – if we could get Jim, the wicket-keeper, out.

I brought the field in close except for two out on the short boundary and I decided to take a risk with Tylan. Three overs passed without a run being scored and Cal came off with brilliant figures.

	Overs	Mdns	Runs	Wkts
C. Sebastien	4	3	2	3

Tylan had an lbw turned down and then bowled an unplayable ball which turned and bounded and lobbed off the batsman's gloves to Cal at short gully. He took an easy catch.

Jim Hunt was still there and he was now joined by the little off-spinner who had taken us apart. He edged Tylan for two and then pushed a quick single round the corner.

They needed four to win with four wickets left. I decided to bowl at Cal's end. Off the third ball, the off-spinner played a slashing shot at one which was moving away from him outside the off-stump. It flew like a bullet to gully where Cal threw himself low to his left. He couldn't hold on to the ball but managed to knock it up two-handed towards Azzie in the slips. Azzie dived and held it but, as his body hit the ground, the ball bounced out. It was a great effort but he flung his cap on the ground in disgust. He knew we hadn't a hope unless we took every chance we got.

Cal was holding his hand with a look of agony on his face; the little finger of his right hand was sticking out at right angles. He'd caught it on the ground as he dived for the catch and the whole weight of his body had landed on it and bent it back. Sid took one look and said it was probably dislocated and Cal'd have to go to hospital to have the finger put back in place.

Before he was rushed away he just had time to see my next ball being swung for four between the two boundary fielders at mid-wicket and square-leg. We'd lost by four wickets.

To make things worse as we walked off, there was Clive standing on the boundary waiting for us with a silly grin on his face. As the Ladies clapped us off the field, he said, "Good thing you picked Ohbert after all, Hooker. How many ducks was it? Six?"

I ignored him and walked over to shake hands with the Ladies' captain. Frankie couldn't keep quiet though. "Well, look who it is," he said. "The leader of the Glory Gardens Supporters Club."

Tylan said, "Hi Clive. Don't let us keep you. You must be

late for something. You usually are."

"True," said Clive. "I've got better things to do than watch a bunch of no-hopers who think they can play cricket." And he swaggered off, laughing and making quacking noises. No one was sorry to see him go.

Everything now hung on the result of the game between the Berks and Stoneyheath. Kiddo told us he'd arranged for someone to phone him from the ground. If the Berks won we were probably out of the Cup, but if Stoneyheath won, our two points from the draw would take us through as runners up.

At 7.30 the phone rang. It was Frankie and Jo's mum ringing to ask when they would be home. Big groan.

Immediately it rang again. Stoneyheath had won by just three runs.

Frankie threw Ohbert's baseball cap in the air and then jumped on it. We were through to the semifinals. But we hadn't deserved it.

HOME TEAM	OUR LADY OF LOURDES v GLORY GARDENS	AWAY TEAM	AT OUR LADY ETC. DATE JUNE 16TH

INNINGS OF GLORY GARDENS .... TOSS WON BY G.G... WEATHER STICKY.

BATSMAN	RUNS SCORED	HOW OUT	BOWLER	SCORE
1 M. ROSE		bowled	HASTE	0
2 C. SEBASTIEN		bowled	CALVERLEY	0
3 A. NAZAR		ct SMITH	CALVERLEY	0
4 E. DAVIES	1.1.1.1	NOT OUT		4
5 J. PADGETT	1.1.	lbw	CALVERLEY	2
6 H. KNIGHT	4	bowled	CALVERLEY	4
7 T. VELLACOTT		RUN OUT		0
8 F. ALLEN		bowled	HASTE	0
9 M. LEAR	1.	ct PARSONS	CALVERLEY	1
10 J. GUNN		st HUNT	McEWAN	0
11 P. BENNETT	1.5.	RUN OUT		6

FALL OF WICKETS

SCORE	0	0	0	5	13	13	14	16	17	23
BAT NO	2	3	1	5	6	7	8	9	10	11

BYES	1.1.	2
L BYES	1.1.1	3
WIDES		
NO BALLS	1.	

TOTAL EXTRAS	6
TOTAL	23
FOR WKTS	10

SCORE AT A GLANCE

BOWLER	BOWLING ANALYSIS ⊙ NO BALL + WIDE	OVS	MDS	RUNS	WKT
1 J. HASTE	M :.w :.. ... / i.1 .. iw/ X	4	1	5	2
2 M. CALVERLEY	W iiw 4w. .w. ⊙.. X	4	1	7	5
3 D. McEWAN	M w.i	2	1	1	1
4 M. PARSONS	M .5.	2	1	5	0
5					
6					
7					
8					
9					

HOME TEAM	OUR LADY OF LOURDES. V GLORY GARDENS	AWAY TEAM	AT OUR LADY DATE JUNE 16TH.

INNINGS OF OUR LADY OF LOURDES... TOSS WON BY G.G.... WEATHER STICKY

BATSMAN	RUNS SCORED	HOW OUT	BOWLER	SCORE
1 O. SMITH	2	bowled	GUNN	2
2 J. HUNT	1.4.1.1.1	NOT	OUT	8
3 M. PARSONS	1	c & b	SEBASTIEN	1
4 R. COTTERALL		ct PADGETT	SEBASTIEN	0
5 J. MAULE		ct NAZAR	SEBASTIEN	0
6 D. O'MAHONEY	1	lbw	GUNN	1
7 D. McEWAN		ct SEBASTIEN	VELLACOTT	0
8 M. CALVERLEY	2.1.4	NOT	OUT	7
9				
10				
11				

FALL OF WICKETS

	1	2	3	4	5	6	7	8	9	10
SCORE	5	11	15	15	16	17				
BAT NO	1	3	4	5	6	7				

BYES	I	
L.BYES		
WIDES	I.I.I.	3
NO BALLS	I	I

TOTAL EXTRAS	5
TOTAL	24
FOR	
WKTS	6

SCORE AT A GLANCE

BOWLING ANALYSIS ⊙ NO BALL + WIDE

BOWLER	1	2	3	4	5	6	7	8	9	10	11	12	13	OVS	MDS	RUNS	WKT
1 M. LEAR			X											2	0	9	0
2 J. GUNN				W	X									4	1	4	2
3 C. SEBASTIEN	W	M	M	X										4	3	2	3
4 T. VELLACOTT	M													2	1	4	1
5 H. KNIGHT														0.4	0	4	0
6																	
7																	
8																	
9																	

Chapter Ten

Stoneyheath & Stockton *beat* **Birtly Parks by three runs**
Our Lady of Lourdes *beat* **Glory Gardens by four wickets**
Wyckham Wanderers *beat* **Lawrence Gubdale by 47 runs**
Mudlarks *beat* **Orchard Pies by 21 runs**

Group 1	W	L	Pts	Group 2	W	L	Pts
Stoneyheath	2	0	10*	Wyckham	3	0	12
Glory Gardens	1	1	6*	Mudlarks	2	1	8
Lady of Lourdes	1	2	4	Orchard P	1	2	4
Birtly Parks	1	2	4	Lawrence Gub	0	3	0

* Rain affected match between Stoneyheath & Stockton and
Glory Gardens. 2 points each.

Semifinals – June 23rd
Stoneyheath & Stockton v Mudlarks
Wyckham Wanderers v Glory Gardens

"I don't care if Wyckham haven't lost a game," said Jo. "We
could have beaten them last time if we'd played properly. And
I've got a funny feeling we will beat them on Wednesday."

"That's not what Liam Katz thinks," said Marty. Marty
told us he'd seen Liam in town and Liam didn't rate our
chances at all.

"He said they were only mucking about in the last game,"
said Marty. "This time it's for real. And they've got a better

team out – they'll be full strength for the semifinal."

We certainly wouldn't be. Cal was definitely out for the next game; his finger was a real mess and the doctor had told him he couldn't play for at least 2 weeks.

"Don't worry, I'll be back for the Big One," he told us.

Fortunately, Cal persuaded Acfield Todd to come to Nets and he said he wanted to play on Wednesday. Clive didn't show up on Saturday morning – not that anyone expected him to. I didn't seriously think he'd play for us again and no one wanted him in the team until he stopped being a bighead. Jacky said that wouldn't happen before he had a brain transplant.

You can probably guess Kiddo's opinion of our performance against the Ladies.

"The whole lot of you put together have got the concentration of a gnat," he said. "Apart from Erica, you batted like headless chickens. Except even a headless chicken knows you've got to wait for the bad ball, doesn't it?"

I wasn't too sure about that – but I think everyone got the message. At Nets, he had us practising forward and backward defensive shots to begin with. He and Wingy, the Firsts' fast bowler, threw balls at us from about six yards away. It was quite good; you really had to concentrate about whether to play back or forward.

After about twenty minutes of that, Kiddo said, "Okay, now I want you to remember two things from this morning. The first is that mostly batsmen get themselves out by playing the wrong shot to the right ball.

He showed how important it was to be in the right position for the shot by demonstrating some of the strokes we had got out to. My favourite was Frankie's leg side pull off the back foot to a ball that was almost a half-volley. Then he demonstrated the front-foot straight-drive he should have played.

"Do you want to know your batting average for Glory Gardens, Francis Allen?" asked Jo.

"Can't wait," said Frankie.

Frankie swings across the line of a well-pitched-up ball and misses completely

This is the shot he should have played – on the front foot and down the line of the delivery.

"1.33 after three rotten innings," said Jo. "That's pathetic."

"I give you permission to leave my scores out of your book if you don't like them," said Frankie.

"Be easier to leave you out of the team," said Jo.

Kiddo's second tip was about what he called attitude. "Don't go out there thinking 'How can I stop this ball hitting my wicket?' What you should be thinking is 'How can I score off it?'"

He showed us what he meant. He asked us all to bowl at him and before each ball bounced he shouted out the shot he was going to play. "Cover drive", "leg glance", "push for one run", "forward defensive". One ball from Tylan turned and took an outside edge as he drove at it. "Caught in the slips," shouted Frankie. Kiddo smiled and said, "Well bowled."

While this was going on we suddenly heard Gatting barking and snarling. If Gatting snarls it's serious because he's usually too fat and lazy to open both eyes at the same time. We looked over to the pavilion and saw a strange sight. A very tall, thin man in a rather scruffy old black coat was trying to kick Gatting, but fat and slow though he is, Gatting had no difficulty in getting out of the way. The kicks were hopelessly badly directed and twice the man fell over backwards as he lost his balance. He was cursing and swearing at the dog.

"Stay here," said Kiddo to us. And he dropped his bat and strode over to the man. Gatting immediately stopped barking and the man turned on Kiddo. They stood face to face for a long time. We couldn't hear what they were saying – Kiddo was standing quite still and the tall man was waving his arms about.

"50p Kiddo lands one on him," said Frankie.

"Oh shut up, idiot," said Jo. "Or I'll land one on you."

Suddenly the man turned round, fell over Gatting, picked himself up and staggered off in a zig-zag path past the pavilion. Kiddo slowly walked back towards us.

"Who was he?" asked Frankie.

"That," said Kiddo, "was Clive's father. It seems Clive's gone missing and he's looking for him. I don't quite know why he's so angry but I do know he's been drinking a bit too much for his own good. I mean anyone who thinks old Gatting is a 'savage, wild beast' must be slightly confused. Well, where was . . . "

There was a sudden crash from the pavilion.

We all rushed over to where the noise had come from. A brick had been thrown through the visitor's changing room window. It didn't take a detective to guess who'd done it, but there was no sign of Clive's dad.

"Call the Riot Squad!" cried Frankie.

Kiddo asked "Do any of you know where Clive lives?"

I looked at Cal and he nodded. He told Kiddo the story of Clive and his dad, although he had no real idea where they lived. "Somewhere on the Lillee Estate, I think my mum said," finished Cal.

"I've got his phone number," I told Kiddo.

"Hmm," said Kiddo. "Best to do nothing hasty, I reckon." And he got a dustpan and brush and swept up the glass.

Later I had a word with Kiddo on his own. I asked him whether he thought we'd been wrong to drop Clive.

"You pick the team, kiddo, not me," he said. Then he smiled and added, "Mind you, he wouldn't get in my team until he got down off his high horse. And that little incident just now has got nothing to do with it, okay?"

That helped a bit but I still wondered whether we had made the right decision.

———————— • ————————

On Tuesday evening I got a call from Jacky Gunn. He told me his gran was seriously ill in Yorkshire and the whole family was going up to see her in hospital. Poor Jacky, I don't know whether he was more upset about missing the match or about his gran. I told him not to worry, that we'd win the game for him and he rang off.

It was too late to find another player – though we tried. I was surprised that even Marty didn't think it was a good idea to ask Clive. "He'd probably refuse to play anyway," he said. "We'd have to find him first," said Azzie.

"Yeah, you can't blame him going into hiding," said Frankie, "the way his old man tosses bricks around."

It was lunchtime on the day of the game and Marty, Azzie, Cal, Frankie, Erica and I were talking in the playground.

"Ten against Wyckham," said Azzie. "We had a stronger team when we played them last time."

"Yeah, you're going to be a bit short of bowlers, Hooker," said Cal.

He wasn't joking. Without Cal and Jacky we only had Marty, me, Erica and Tylan. I'd have to risk Jason or Matt or maybe Acfield – he'd bowled one or two good balls in the nets but the rest of them had been rubbish.

"Can't you bowl left-handed, Cal?" said Erica.

"No," said Cal. "And I definitely can't bowl with the right." He took his finger out of the protective sheath and showed it to us. It was about twice its normal size and dark blue.

"It looks like a sausage that's gone off," said Azzie.

"Give us a bite," said Frankie.

Cal winced. "I tried holding a ball but I can't grip anything. And anyway my mum's told Kiddo not to let me play, 'cos she knows I want to."

"Talking of fingers, do you think old Fingers Whitestick will be umpiring for them?" said Marty.

"Oh no, I'd forgotten about him," said Erica.

"Don't let the ball hit your pads whatever you do," said Marty.

"The Glory Gardens Ten versus the Wyckham Twelve," said Azzie.

"Well if he is umpiring, he's in for a surprise," said Cal.

And although we kept asking him what he meant he wouldn't say any more about it.

Chapter Eleven

The first person we saw when we arrived at Wyckham's ground was Fingers. He was fussing about putting up some deck chairs outside the pavilion.

He scowled at us as we walked past.

Cal said, "Good evening, Mr Whitehouse," rather insincerely, and sat down in one of the deck chairs.

"At least he won't have the fun of giving me out today," he said in a sort of whisper to Marty – but loud enough for the Whitestick to hear.

Liam came over and we walked out to toss.

I told him we'd only got ten players and he pretended to be sorry about it. But you could tell he was really rather pleased.

"We've got our best side out for the first time this year," he said. He also told me they hadn't lost yet – as if I didn't know. "And I got 50 against Mudlarks and Lawrence Gubdale," he said.

"But Lawrence Gubdale are rabbits, aren't they? Anyone could get 50 against them." I'd had enough of all this Wyckham Wanderers boasting.

He didn't answer *and* he lost the toss. Heads again. I told him we'd bat. With our bowling, I thought the best bet was to try and set them a big target and hope they'd get careless going for it.

I remembered that Jason hadn't liked batting against Win Reifer, their opening bowler, so I decided I'd ask Erica to open. She was happy to have a go. I told her and Matt to go easy to begin with and watch out for Fingers. I thought I'd bat at four, after Azzie, and put Jason in at five.

Win Reifer opened up with a very quick over against Matt. A couple missed the off-stump by inches but he also gave away four byes and a wide. The bowler at the other end was new to us. He wasn't quite as quick as Reifer, but he bowled straight and got the ball to bounce. He looked good.

Erica and Matt stuck to it and survived the opening overs. There were a couple of appeals for lbw but they were at Sid's end and he shook his head both times. None of us were in any doubt that Fingers would have given them out. The runs were coming quite quickly too, because Reifer was bowling a lot of wides. Erica played a delicate leg glance for two and Matt edged two twos in succession all along the ground through the slips.

Then Erica got a beauty from the new opening bowler, Thackeray. It bounced on middle stump and lifted. She played back but it grazed her top glove as it went through to Charlie Gale behind the stumps. 16 for one. Not a bad start.

Azzie went off like a rocket. He played two perfectly timed cuts against Reifer and then he edged the next ball to Liam at first slip. He dived forward and held it in both hands. "Owzthat!" screamed Reifer and Charlie Gale. "Out!" said Fingers, almost before the appeal had begun and I swear he was smiling. Then there was a short silence, but as Azzie began to walk someone said, "Not out."

It was Liam. The ball hadn't carried and he'd taken the catch on the bounce. Fingers looked really disappointed but there was nothing he could do. I know Liam's not a cheat but it would have been easy for him to say nothing. Sid told us afterwards that he'd seen the 'catch' clearly from square-leg and he'd have given it not out. But I think he was quite relieved he hadn't had to overrule Fingers.

Azzie whacked the next ball through the covers for three which must have made Reifer really pleased.

After eight overs Liam brought himself on to bowl and

immediately trapped Matt leg before. It looked fairly close, but he had no chance anyway against the Whitestick. Up went the Finger.

I walked to the wicket trying to think what I should say to Azzie. I told him I'd try and keep one end tight while he played his natural game.

I got off the mark with a two off my legs. For a terrible moment I thought I was going to miss the ball and let it hit my pads. That would have been instant death. But it went with a nice sweet feel off the middle of the bat. As always I felt a lot better after scoring a couple of runs. I looked up at the score-board; we were 29 for two off nine overs.

I scored one more run in the next three overs. But Azzie added 15 to his score. As usual, he wasn't slogging. He timed and placed his shots so well that little pushes were going for twos. Even Liam applauded a pull shot played all along the ground in front of square for four.

I could hear Frankie shouting from the boundary, "Azzie 24, Hooker 3. Come on, Hooker. You're allowed to score runs, too."

I wasn't worried. If we carried on scoring at five runs an over we'd finish with 80 or more. That was a good target.

I remembered something Kiddo had said to me. "Build your innings in fives – aim to get five runs, then ten. Don't worry about the big targets – they'll come."

Liam was running up to bowl the next ball to me. Just as his arm came over there was an extraordinary noise like a crash of cymbals from his right. Fingers had sneezed. Well it wasn't so much a sneeze as an explosion. Liam jumped two feet in the air. The ball lobbed out of his hand and bounced down the pitch. I stepped out to meet it and hit it on the second bounce between mid-wicket and square-leg for four.

There was a silence, followed by an enormous cheer from the boundary and then an even louder sneeze from Whitestick. He had gone bright purply red and he was gasping for breath. Another sneeze.

Eventually, Azzie turned to him and said very quietly but with an enormous grin, "Aren't you going to signal that four, Mr Whitehouse?" By now tears were running down Finger's nose and he kept bending double every time he sneezed. In between sneezes he sort of bounced up and down making little 'whooping' noises – 'whoop, whoop, whup, whup, ACHHAAAAAGH!'

And each time he sneezed another huge cheer went up from the Glory Gardens bench. I heard Frankie shout, "Sorry umpire, the scorer doesn't understand that signal." Even the Wyckham players were beginning to laugh. Sid came over and tried to look serious and in the end he had to help Fingers, still sneezing, off the pitch.

One of the Wyckham senior team players came on as reserve umpire. And Liam continued his over. Now and again there was another huge explosion from the direction of the pavilion and another roar of laughter led by Frankie and Cal.

Azzie was out caught and bowled for 29 and he was clapped all the way to the boundary. It had been a brilliant innings.

I decided we might as well keep attacking and told Jason to run for everything. It could have been a mistake to say that because he ran me out next over going for a second run. But I didn't mind – well, not too much. 59 on the board and we had Wyckham on the run if we kept up the pressure. "Don't go mad, but take every run you can," I said to Tylan as I passed him.

Tylan didn't get a duck. His first run got the biggest cheer of the day from the Glory Gardens gang. Or maybe not quite the biggest, that went to Fingers' sneeze.

We began the last four overs on 68. Jason was bowled going for a big heave and in came Frankie. The next five balls went for 4; 2; 2; 4; 2 – every one swung ferociously on the leg side. He tonked one from a foot outside the off-stump and it went for four through mid-wicket. I saw Kiddo sigh and put his head in his hands.

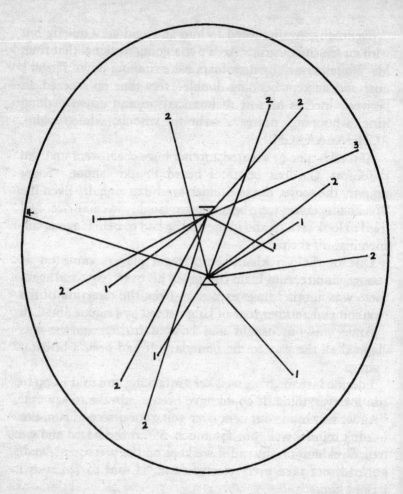

Jo's 'batogram' shows where Azzie scores his 29 runs. As you can see he plays his shots all round the wicket but a lot of his runs come in the cover area.

There was nothing the bowler could do about it. He wasn't even bowling badly. It was just that Frankie's swings were catching every ball in the middle of the bat and although all his shots were in the air, they kept bouncing out of reach of the fielders. 14 off the over. 82 for five. With three overs to go we could score a hundred.

Frankie took one swing too many and was bowled round his legs next over. Acfield had just one swing, missed and he was bowled, too. Marty avoided the hat trick and he and Tylan added another six before Marty was caught at square-leg, also going for a swing down the leg side. That brought in Ohbert with eight balls to go. We were on 91.

Tylan walked down the wicket and had a word with Ohbert. Watching from the boundary, we couldn't see the point. Talking tactics to Ohbert was like trying to teach your budgie to do maths. He might hear what you say. He might even be able to repeat it after a bit. But he won't have a clue what you're talking about.

Ohbert played his forward defensive shot and ran at the same time. Somehow the ball squirted off the bat and they got an easy single. Tylan managed to keep the bowling for the final over and then score two twos and a single. 98 and two balls left and Ohbert to face. He missed the first by miles. It was the forward defensive shot and the ball went down the leg side. The final ball was a bit short and Ohbert played his other shot swinging into it with all his strength. The ball lobbed just over the bowler's head. Ohbert looked around to see where it had gone and, with Tylan screaming at him, eventually set off for a run. Tylan passed him before he had gone three strides and turned for the second run. They arrived at the bowler's crease at exactly the same time. Tylan had finished his second run; Ohbert his first. The ball was thrown in to the bowler and he took the bails off. But both batsmen were in the crease.

"Oh but . . . " stammered Ohbert.

"Get down the other end," screamed Tylan.

Ohbert went off like a wild thing, his bat above his head.

All the bowler had to do was underarm the ball to the keeper and Ohbert would be run out by a mile. But he threw it hard. The keeper fumbled and dropped it. He picked it up and desperately lunged at the wicket. But Ohbert was through like an express train. He let out a great cry of joy and threw his bat miles in the air. And then ducked. It missed him by a couple of centimetres as it came down.

We'd scored 100. Who'd have believed it?

Chapter Twelve

Cal came into the changing room, took one look at Frankie and burst out laughing. There were tears running down his face and he could hardly speak.

"What's the matter with him?" asked Marty.

"Don't ask. He's probably just pleased we've scored a century without him," said Tylan.

"Yeah, our first ton," said Frankie. "That's nothing to sneeze at." And he and Cal collapsed on the floor with another attack of snorts and giggles.

"Okay," I said. "What's going on?"

"Are you going to tell them?" Frankie asked Cal.

"Oh, all right," gasped Cal. "Well, you know how Fingers is all the time wiping his face and blowing his nose with his snotrag?"

"Yeah, so what?" said Marty.

"Well, we just mixed up a little surprise for him, didn't we? And then we kind of sprinkled it in the pocket of one of the umpire's coats."

"I thought he was never going to blow his nose," said Frankie.

"Sneezing powder?" said Azzie.

"The best. Home-made and twice as strong!" said Cal.

The row in our changing room could have been heard for miles around. We were late going out to field – Frankie couldn't do his keeper's pads up because he was still shaking with laughter and Cal had to tell the story again to Ohbert because he had his Walkman on the first time.

When we emerged from the changing room, the two umpires were waiting for us. And, yes, Fingers was back. His eyes looked a bit red but he had stopped sneezing. He must have known something was up from all the chuckling and sniggering.

The last thing Glory Gardens were thinking about was the cricket. They'd all relaxed because we'd scored so many runs and they'd forgotten, with our bowling attack, even a hundred wasn't enough. I hadn't.

Somehow I had to bowl Jason or possibly Acfield, without them getting absolutely slaughtered. I wanted to open with me and Marty, but I thought I'd try and bring Jason on after a couple of overs.

The bowling was all right to begin with – in fact, I thought I bowled pretty well – but the fielding was terrible. Frankie dropped a catch off me and Tylan let a ball go between his legs for four as he didn't get his body behind the ball.

This is how he should have fielded it. It is called the long barrier.

We must have given away more than half the runs they scored in the first four overs. They were already on 21 and the openers were going well.

I didn't dare bowl Marty any more, because I wanted to keep him back for a couple of overs later on if they got completely on top. So I went for a double change, Tylan and Erica.

"Come on liven up, Glory Gardens," shouted Cal from the boundary, clapping his hands. "You're slower than old Gatting." Gatting heard his name. He got up slowly, walked over to Cal and gave him a big lick.

Erica bowled – a short one down the leg side – and it was swung by Wood, the bigger of the two openers, hard and straight at Jason at square-leg. It would have gone straight through him if he hadn't got his hands there. But the ball stuck. It was a magnificent catch.

Erica rushed over to him. "Brilliant catch."

"Thanks," said Jason blushing and blowing on his fingers to cool them down.

In came Liam and immediately he looked in a class of his own. Tylan got the other opener, though, with a good turning and lifting leg break which bounced off the shoulder of his bat to Azzie in the slips.

Erica had a very good lbw appeal turned down by you-know-who. But after eight overs, they were 38 for two. Liam had already scored eleven and he'd only faced ten balls.

I knew I had to bring Jason on . . . but Liam would murder him. Nothing for it though. I asked him to bowl at Tylan's end.

His first two balls were wides. Then Liam hit a long hop for four through mid-wicket. So what happened next was quite amazing. Jason bowled from wide of the stumps – a slightly quicker ball. It pitched on middle and off-stump at an awkward length which had Liam playing forward and then back. It must have straightened off the pitch because it beat the outside edge of Liam's straight backward defensive stroke and hit

Jason bowls a ball of full length which has Liam uncertain whether to play forward or back. In the end he plays back, when he should have played forward, and is clean bowled.

the off-stump half way up. Unbelievable! Jason had bowled the best batsman on the field – with a beaut.

In her last over, Erica bowled Charlie Gale for a duck. They had exactly 50 for four and we'd bowled half our overs.

I replaced Erica at the Fingers end and I immediately had a really good lbw rejected. The very next ball took out the middle stump. "Owzthat, then!" I screamed at Whitestick. I don't think he was too pleased.

Five wickets down. But they were still going for it – no doubt about that. Reifer came in looking very, very determined and hit some big blows against my bowling and then, an enormous swing for four off Jason. He looked extremely dangerous. But Jason came to the rescue again with his second perfect delivery. This time the ball cut away even more. It pitched middle and hit the outside of the off-stump. Win Reifer scowled, looked at his wicket and then said, "Good ball," to Jason before stalking off.

Jason's three overs had cost us 20 runs – including six wides – but he'd got rid of their two most dangerous batsmen.

I got another wicket in my final over. A good catch behind by Frankie to make up for his earlier drop off me. So I finished with 2 for thirteen.

The end came quickly. Jason took a third wicket. This time it was an awful long hop skied to Matt out at deep mid-wicket where he took a good catch. Jason deserved that one.

I brought back Marty and he took two wickets in three balls. A straight yorker knocked over the middle and leg stumps. Then a hard low caught and bowled chance which he picked up one-handed by his left foot. They were all out for 75.

Frankie pulled out a stump and set off for the boundary waving it wildly over his head and shouting, "Glory, Glory, Hallelujah. We're in the Final. We're in the Final!"

"Well bowled, Jacey," said Cal, who'd rushed on to the pitch to congratulate us. "I've never seen you bowl like that in the nets. What's the secret?"

Jason grinned. "Dunno. I think the first one slipped," he said.

As we walked off I just caught sight of a figure over by the woods on the far boundary. A tall boy in a raggedy tee-shirt and jeans. He looked like a tramp but there was something familiar about him. Then I realised – it was Clive. He saw me looking at him and disappeared into the trees.

Before I could think what to do Liam came over and shook hands. He looked really sick but he didn't make any excuses. "Well played," he said. "You scored too many runs for us."

Kiddo was delighted. I'd never seen him excited like that. "If you were all a few years older I'd say the beers are on me," he said.

I told him I'd just seen Clive.

"I'm getting worried about that boy," said Kiddo. "If he's sleeping rough the police will have to hear about it. I reckon I'll call in and have a chat with them this evening." He slapped me on the back. "But first we've got some celebrating to do. You were brilliant."

I couldn't argue with that. As Frankie said, "WE'RE IN THE FINAL!"

HOME TEAM	WYCKHAM WNDRS	v GLORY GARDENS	AWAY TEAM	AT WYCKHAM DATE JUNE 23RD

INNINGS OF GLORY GARDENS........   TOSS WON BY G.G.... WEATHER SUNNY.

BATSMAN	RUNS SCORED	HOW OUT	BOWLER	SCORE
1 M. ROSE	1.2.2.1	lbw	KATZ	6
2 E. DAVIES	2.	ct GALE	THACKERAY	2
3 A. NAZAR	1.2.2.3.1.2.2.1.1.2.1.4.2.2.1.2	ck b	PRESTON	29
4 H. KNIGHT	2.1.4.1.1.	RUN	OUT	9
5 J. PADGETT	1.1.1.1.1.1.1.1	bowled	T. WOOD	8
6 T. VELLACOTT	1.1.1.2.1.2.2.1	NOT	OUT	13
7 F. ALLEN	4.2.2.4.2.2	bowled	BUTT	16
8 A. TODD		bowled	BUTT	0
9 M. LEAR	1	ct TATE	J. WOOD	1
10 P. BENNETT	1.2	NOT	OUT	3
11				

FALL OF WICKETS

SCORE	16	27	55	59	68	85	85	91	9	10
	1	2	3	4	5	6	7	8		
BAT NO	2	1	3	4	5	7	8	9		

BYES	4.		4
L.BYES	1.1		2
WIDES	1.1.1.1.1.1.1		7
NO BALLS			

TOTAL EXTRAS	13
TOTAL FOR	100
WKTS	8

SCORE AT A GLANCE

BOWLING ANALYSIS ⊙ NO BALL + WIDE

BOWLER	1	2	3	4	5	6	7	8	9	10	11	12	13	OVS	MDS	RUNS	WKT
1 W. REIFER	··	·+·	·+	22·										4	0	18	0
	·+·	+2	22·	3+··													
2 D. THACKERAY	M	··	··											4	1	4	1
		i··	W·	·i	·i												
3 L. KATZ	·w·	1··	4·1·	··										4	0	19	1
	·2·	121	2·	111													
4 P. PRESTON	·2·	4··	2·W	1+1										4	0	22	1
	2·1	2··	111	1+11													
5 T. WOOD	W42													1	0	14	1
	242																
6 J. BUTT	·12	2·2												2	0	10	2
	WW	1·2															
7 J. WOOD	121													1	0	7	1
	+W11																
8																	
9																	

HOME TEAM	WYCKHAM WNDRS V GLORY GARDENS	AWAY TEAM	AT WYCKHAM	DATE JUNE 23RD

INNINGS OF WYCKHAM WANDERERS.   TOSS WON BY GG WEATHER SUNNY

BATSMAN	RUNS SCORED	HOW OUT	BOWLER	SCORE
1 A. WOOD	2.1.1.4.2.1	ct PADGETT	DAVIES	11
2 K. BASKIN	1.1.2.2.	ct NAZAR	VELLACOTT	6
3 L. KATZ	2.1.2.1.2.1.3.2.1.4	bowled	PADGETT	19
4 B. TATE	1.2.1.2.1	bowled	KNIGHT	7
5 C. GALE		bowled	DAVIES	0
6 R. RAWLINSON	1.1.1.1	ct ALLEN	KNIGHT	4
7 W. REIFER	2.1.4.1	bowled	PADGETT	8
8 J. BUTT		ct ROSE	PADGETT	0
9 T. WOOD	1.2.1	bowled	LEAR	4
10 D. THAKERAY		c & b	LEAR	0
11 P. PRESTON	1.	NOT	OUT	1

FALL OF WICKETS

SCORE	21	28	48	50	57	67	69	74	74	75
BAT NO	1	2	3	5	4	7	6	8	9	10

BYES 1.	1
L BYES 1.1.1.1	4
WIDES 1.1.1.1.1.1.1.1	8
NO BALLS 1.1.	2

TOTAL EXTRAS	15
TOTAL FOR WKTS	75 10

SCORE AT A GLANCE

BOWLING ANALYSIS ⊙ NO BALL + WIDE

BOWLER	1	2	3	4	5	6	7	8	9	10	11	12	13	OVS	MDS	RUNS	WKT
1 M. LEAR	..2.4. / .11 2..	W												2.3	0	11	2
2 H. KNIGHT	.1.⊙. / .1.1.33	.. W 1.. / 2.1 W.1												4	0	13	2
3 E. DAVIES	.W.2.1. / 2.1.⊙..	..2. / .11 ⊙.1												4	0	12	2
4 T. VELLACOTT	2.1.3. / ..W1.2													2	0	10	1
5 J. PADGETT	.+4 0+. .41 .2. / ⊙... +2 ⊙..⊙..													4	0	24	3
6																	
7																	
8																	
9																	

Chapter Thirteen

On Saturday morning everyone was at Nets. Jacky was back from Yorkshire; his gran was a lot better. Acfield was there, too. And Ohbert. In fact, the only Glory Gardens player missing was Jason who was on knicker duty.

The Final was against Mudlarks; they'd beaten Stoneyheath off the last ball of the match. We didn't know much about them, except Liam Katz told me they were good. He reckoned they had a good left-handed bat called Henry Rossi and their captain was the best wicket-keeper Liam had ever seen. He'd got three stumpings in the game against Wyckham. Wyckham had only beaten them because Liam had got a 'brilliant fifty'. At least, that's what he said.

We'd been practising for less than ten minutes and I was bowling to Azzie, when suddenly everyone went quiet. I looked up and saw Clive walking over towards me.

He was wearing the same old tee-shirt and grubby jeans I'd seen him in on Wednesday and he looked as if he'd been sleeping in them for days.

"Sorry about what I said after the game the other day," he said to me rather quietly. You could tell he'd been rehearsing his words and they didn't sound very convincing. But I couldn't believe it. Clive apologising!

Frankie started to say something but Cal lobbed a cricket ball at him which hit him somewhere soft and painful. "Ow!" yelled Frankie. "Who did that?"

Clive looked dreadful. He looked as though he hadn't

washed for a week or slept much for that matter. He had big black circles under his eyes and he seemed thinner and somehow older. It was obvious he'd come to Nets only because he wanted to play in the Final. But it was a big thing for him to apologise – he had a lot of pride to swallow.

I chucked my ball to him. "Forget it," I said.

He hardly said another word during practice. He bowled accurately and quite quickly – then batted beautifully as usual. I'd almost forgotten how good he was.

I could see Kiddo keeping an eye on him but he didn't say anything except, "Hello, Clive. Things okay?"

Of course, everyone wanted to ask about his old man but even Frankie got the message that Clive hadn't come to talk. I began to wonder whether he even knew about last Saturday's 'incident'. In the end Kiddo hadn't called the police about it and the window was already mended. But were the cops out hunting for Clive at this very moment? Had Kiddo been to the police station to report him missing?

After Nets, Kiddo walked over to Clive and they had a long talk on their own. Then he called us all together for a 'team chat' which was pretty boring. But after that he showed us a video he'd taken of our game against Wyckham and some bits he'd filmed in the Nets.

We booed Fingers for giving Azzie out caught in the slips, cheered Azzie's great pull for four and groaned at some of our fielding. I was pleased with my bowling and got Kiddo to do a slow-motion replay of the one Frankie caught off me. But the best moment was Jason's amazing over against Liam. (Unfortunately Kiddo hadn't filmed Fingers' sneezing explosion.)

"Look at that fielding," Kiddo kept saying. "Look at Tylan there. See? He's not walking in when the ball's being bowled. And see that? Matthew's not backing up at all."

When the video had finished Kiddo told us to make sure we all enjoyed the Final and not to worry too much if we lost (which, of course, we weren't going to).

Matthew isn't backing up. If Frankie misses Erica's throw it'll go for overthrows. This is where Matt should be fielding.

Ohbert came up to me, "About this Final, Hooker," he said. "You know I won't mind being dropped if you've got someone better. I mean, I will mind . . . er, but I want the team to win and if you think . . . Oh but, you know."

It was the longest speech I'd ever heard from Ohbert and I could tell he was desperate to play. Who'd have thought old Ohbert would have cared so much. I told him we were going to pick the team straight away and he'd be the first to know our decision.

Half an hour later Jo, Marty and I were sitting round the table in the Club kitchen. There was a sheet of paper in front of us which we'd been staring at for ages.

Definites

1	Hooker Knight	8	Frankie Allen
2	Marty Lear	9	Tylan Vellacott
3	Azzie Nazar	10	Matt Rose
4	Erica Davis	11	?
5	Cal Sebastien (IF FIT)		(from) Clive da Costa
6	Jacky Gunn		Acfield Todd
7	Jason Padgett		Ohbert Bennett

"Well, I don't think you can just dump Ohbert for the Final," said Jo.

"Even if he's hopeless?" said Marty.

"He's better than he used to be," I said feebly. But we were getting nowhere.

Jo looked at me. "You'll have to decide," she said. "I'm for Ohbert. Marty thinks Clive should play, as usual."

"Well I agree Acfield's the third choice," I said. "Even though he's a better cricketer than Ohbert."

"Then we should play Ohbert even though Clive's better than him," said Jo.

"Might as well play with ten again," mumbled Marty.

I looked at them both. "Trouble with Clive," I said, "is that he'll probably upset the whole team. Just because he's turned up to Nets once and apologised doesn't mean he's changed."

"So?"

"So I think we should play Ohbert and make Clive first reserve."

It was agreed and we wrote out the team for the Final.

When we emerged from the kitchen, everyone was still hanging around.

"Here comes the judge, here comes the judge," sang Frankie.

Jo told him we'd chosen a new wicket-keeper and Frankie believed her. He rushed up to look at the team sheet as Jo pinned it up on the Club notice-board.

Everyone gathered round to look except Ohbert who was listening to his Walkman. I went and told him he was playing and, when he finally heard what I was saying, a big smile spread over his face.

"Oh but . . . that's great, Hooker. But . . . "

Acfield came up to me and said he understood and he'd come along to support us. Clive was standing on his own. I went over to him.

"Sorry, Clive," I said. "It wasn't easy."

"Yeah," he said.

There was a long silence and he stared at me. Then he turned and just walked away. I think he was really disappointed and didn't want anyone to see how upset he was. I noticed Kiddo following him out of the pavilion.

But that wasn't the end of the selection drama – not by a long way.

On Tuesday evening I got a phone call from Matt's mother to tell me that Matt had 'flu and he was in bed. He'd been sent home from school and she didn't think there was a chance he'd be able to play. As Matt didn't go to our school, this was the first I'd heard of the bad news.

What was I going to do now? Clive was first reserve – so should I ring him? But what if his dad answered the phone? It didn't look like Clive was living at home anyway. I felt stupid that I hadn't asked him how I could get in touch with him – but then he hadn't given me much of a chance rushing off like that. In the end I did phone but there was no one there. I rang him again on Wednesday morning. Still no reply.

When I got to school I saw Kiddo and he said he'd try and get hold of Clive at his school. "That's if he's there – he's not been putting in too many appearances recently."

Kiddo told me Clive was now living with his aunt. "He's been having a really tough time with his father," he said. "Comes home drunk every night and just smashes the place up. In the end Clive decided he'd had enough and he left home. He took some of his father's money and walked out. Seems he's been living in a shed in Brearley Wood for over a week."

"Did he know about his dad smashing the pavilion window?" I asked.

"No, that was quite funny. When I told him he offered to pay for it with his father's money. He's not a bad lad really, you know. If only his father could be made to see sense."

I couldn't wait to tell Cal. When I saw him he stuck his finger under my nose.

"Oh no, don't tell me you can't play," I said.

"There's been a lot of arguing about this in the Sebastien household," he said, pulling the famous finger out of its black sheath and showing me. It was still very swollen.

"Can you play?" I asked again.

"According to my mum, no. But my dad and I say yes. I've tried holding a bat and it's a bit painful. But it's only the little finger, so it shouldn't affect my bowling."

That was a relief. I told him about Matt and the Clive story so far.

Cal said, "That's no problem. Acfield's got his kit. He'll play if Clive doesn't turn up."

Good start to the Big Match – I didn't even know who was playing. Typical Glory Gardens.

Chapter Fourteen

Clive was at the ground when we arrived.

"You're playing," I said. "Matt's sick."

"Brilliant!" he said. He wasn't just pleased, he was really excited. All right, he wasn't too bothered about Matt but something about him was different. For a start he looked better – he was wearing a clean polo shirt and new tracksuit bottoms. But that wasn't all of it. I'd never seen Clive like this before; he was usually so cool and arrogant. I began to wonder if we'd got him wrong – just a bit.

Then he said, "I suppose you'll want me to open the batting?"

"Yeah, you're so good you'd better open both ends," said Frankie.

Another surprise. Clive just smiled and said nothing.

I'd worked out a batting order if Clive was playing. It went:

Jason Padgett	Tylan Vellacott
Erica Davis	Cal Sebastien
Azzie Nazar	Marty Lear
Clive da Costa	Jacky Gunn
Hooker Knight (capt.)	Ohbert Bennett
Frankie Allen	

I'd put Cal down the order because of his finger. Opening with Jason and Erica would have been crazy a couple of weeks ago. But now they seemed to be getting on so well that it was the obvious choice. Jason was still a bit suspect against fast, short-pitched bowling but I was just hoping they had no one as quick as Win Reifer.

I tossed and lost (heads again!) and the Mudlarks' captain chose to bat. I wasn't too unhappy about that because fielding first would give us a chance to get over our nerves.

In the changing room everyone was really excited. We'd never played in front of a 'crowd' before. There were at least fifty spectators. Even my sister had come to watch – I'd spent the whole week trying to answer her daft questions about what she called 'those silly cricket rules' and I knew she still didn't understand anything. I knew it for certain when she said to me at breakfast, "If a fielder catches the ball without it bouncing, how many runs does he get?"

"Six," I said, to keep her quiet.

Tylan's dad had come in the old, blue van he used for the knicker stall. It was really dirty and someone had written 'By appointment, Knickers to the Queen' on the side of it. He came into the changing room and wished us luck, which was nice of him. He told Ohbert he was looking forward to working with him again and handed him a pair of 'lucky' yellow and green boxers to wear for the big match. Ohbert said, "Oh but . . . thanks," and Tylan's dad gave him a big slap on the back. Ohbert fell over the kit bag and struggled to his feet looking pleased and embarrassed at the same time.

The game got off to a slow start. Marty and Jacky bowled well and the Mudlarks openers weren't taking any chances. Our fielding was keen, too. Cal nearly got a run out with a throw in from the covers and even Ohbert was running to back up the throws to the keeper. I was able to keep a tight ring of fielders saving singles with only one out on the boundary.

After five overs they'd scored just 12 runs. I decided to take Marty off, so he would have two overs left for the end of the innings, and bowl myself from his end. The first ball I bowled was a bit loose and wide of the off-stump and the batsman took a swing at it. He mistimed it and it just lobbed over Erica's head at extra-cover.

"What about dropping the field back a bit?" said Marty handing me the ball which he'd been polishing up for me.

"Give it a bit longer," I said.

With the field set close, I thought Mudlarks would have to hit the ball through them or over the top if they wanted to speed up the scoring. The openers were showing signs of getting a bit anxious and the Mudlarks supporters were already shouting at them to get on with it.

Sure enough, off the last ball of my over, the batsman went for an ungainly swing over mid-wicket. He got a top edge and the ball lobbed high to Marty at mid-on who caught it without having to move.

"Okay, you win," said Marty, chucking the ball to me with a big grin on his face.

"Nice field placing, Hooker," shouted Frankie.

"Six!" screamed my sister from the boundary.

That brought in Rossi, the left-hander who Liam Katz had warned us about.

I had a fielding plan worked out for him but it was rather complicated because it meant every fielder had to move when the left-hander and right-hander changed ends. And I had to watch them all to make sure they remembered where they were supposed to be after every ball.

Ohbert had the furthest to walk – from short third-man to deep fine-leg. And, sure enough, he was the one we had to keep shouting at because he'd forgotten to change over. My idea was to keep the ring of close fielders for the opener and drop back three – long-on, deep mid-wicket and third-man – for Henry Rossi.

Jacky finished his four overs. He hadn't taken a wicket but he'd only given away nine runs. I brought on Erica to try and keep it tight and put the pressure on them.

The two batsmen were talking in the middle of the pitch and looking at Erica. I heard the opener say, "It's that girl coming on to bowl – must be some easy runs now."

Jason heard them, too. "I shouldn't bet on it, mate," he said

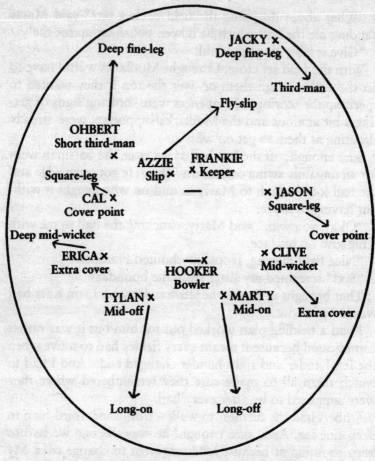

The field changes for left and right-hand bowlers.

as he walked past them. "Watch out for her bouncer!"

Erica had a bit of a problem with the left- and right-hand bat combination to begin with. Her direction wasn't as good as usual especially to the left-hander and Rossi took full advantage of some loose balls down the leg side.

But with the last ball of her second over she knocked out the opener's middle stump.

As he walked back to the pavilion he passed Jason. "What

a shame," said Jace. "Tut tut! Bowled by a girl – whatever will they say?" Three weeks ago Jason would have died before saying anything like that. I think Erica was still a bit confused by the sudden change. The rest of us thought it was a big laugh but Jason didn't seem to notice.

My last over was the best I'd ever bowled for the Gardens. The first ball had Henri Rossi completely beaten outside the off-stump. The next he edged to where slip would have been for a lucky single. Then I had the other batsman plumb lbw but Sid gave it not out. It didn't matter because my next ball came back off the pitch between bat and pad and took out the middle and leg stumps. That's a lovely feeling for a bowler, one stump standing and the other two lying flat on the ground.

I had two balls left. I tried a slower one and the new batsman missed it completely; it bounced just over the wicket. I decided to try and bowl a really fast yorker for the last delivery. I really let it go and the batsman played forward but he was beaten for pace and the ball cannoned into his back pad. Up went Frankie with an enormous appeal.

"OOOOWZTHAAAAT!"

I swung round to see Sid's finger pointing at the batsman. 38 for four. That was more like it – now we had them on the run.

There were eight overs to go but Rossi was still there and playing well. He clouted a two through the covers off Erica. Then he hit a big four to the right of square-leg. I was getting worried about him so I decided to take Erica off next over. Meanwhile I'd brought on Cal at my end. He hadn't bowled since the Ladies' game but he'd been brilliant there.

Rossi hammered him. I think Cal's finger was troubling him. Anyway he couldn't find the length and the left-hander was merciless on anything short. His over cost us ten runs and at the end of it he chucked the ball to me and said grimly, "That's enough of that. Get someone else on who can bowl."

It was time to bring back Marty to calm things down.

They'd raced to 55 for four and with six overs left they were threatening to take us apart. I couldn't risk holding back Marty any longer. It worked. He didn't get Henry Rossi but he had the new batsman caught behind. A brilliant diving catch to his left by Frankie. As he hit the ground the ball bounced out of his glove but somehow he managed to catch it again. He lay there with a big grin on his face.

"Easy peasy," he said.

"I'm going to give Clive a go at your end," I said to Cal.

"Good idea," said Cal with a smile. I told you Cal never broods about things. He bowls a hopeless over and a couple of minutes later he's forgotten all about it. I wish I could do that.

Clive was pleased to get a chance to bowl and he immediately started changing the field I'd set. I moved them all back and told Clive I'd look after the fielders; he could just worry about his bowling. His first ball was a full toss which Rossi hit for three past square-leg. But after that he got a surprising amount of life out of the pitch and was unlucky not to take a wicket with a top edge which bounced just short of Azzie at fly-slip.

Marty bowled his last over for three and I looked around to see who I'd got left to bowl. Tylan? Perhaps Jason? Or maybe bring back Erica for her fourth over?

They were 64 for five when Clive bowled Henri Rossi with a good straight ball. Rossi was going for a big lofted drive and played over the top of the ball which just nicked his off-stump. He'd scored 38 out of 64 – a great knock.

With Rossi out I felt happier about bowling Tylan at the other end but I knew there was always the risk of a leg break bowler giving away a lot of runs, although Tylan had been pretty tidy in the last two games. He was the seventh bowler I'd used today.

His first five balls went for five singles. But with the last he got a bit of extra turn. The batsman went to swing it over extra-cover but got an outside edge. The ball looped high in the air straight towards . . . Ohbert.

Ohbert stood paralysed. Then he suddenly noticed it was a catch. He ran forwards shouting, "Oooh, mine." Then he realised he'd come in too far and ran back. That was followed by a stagger to the right and a short run to the left. It looked as though the ball was dropping well out of his reach, but, at the last second he made a remarkable swooping dive forward and to his right and snatched the ball up in one hand, inches above the grass. He was completely winded as he fell but he managed to grunt, "Owzthat!"

We were all exhausted from just watching. Another amazing Ohbert catch! Even Frankie was speechless for a couple of moments. Through the silence I heard my sister shouting, "Six! Six! Six!"

Ohbert pulled himself to his feet, looked around and said, "Easy peasy." Even the batsman had to laugh.

Clive bowled the last over and got a second wicket from a full toss which was swung straight at Ohbert. And he caught it as if he'd been taking catches all his life.

"Well caught," shouted Clive. And Ohbert beamed and he took another look at the ball in his hand as if he couldn't quite believe it either.

We got our ninth wicket with a run out off the last ball. They tried to run a single to the keeper and Frankie pulled off his right glove and threw down the stumps. Mudlarks finished on 76 for nine. A pretty good total but not huge. We'd bowled and fielded well.

Kiddo was pleased, too. "I reckon you've given yourselves a good chance of winning," he said. "You must have saved twenty runs in the field. That's the best I've seen yet."

"And what about Ohbert," I said.

"Who?" said Kiddo.

"Er, Paul Bennett," I said.

"Well . . . er, amazing!" said Kiddo.

Chapter Fifteen

People show they're nervous in different ways. Frankie and Azzie just talked a lot without making a great deal of sense – which in Frankie's case wasn't very different from usual. Erica went for a walk. Clive sat in the corner of the changing room and didn't say anything. Ohbert fiddled with his Walkman. Jason just looked sick.

I tried to say things like "If we're calm and keep our heads, we can win this." But I knew I was sounding like Kiddo and no one was taking any notice of me.

Cal and I threw a few practice balls at Erica and Jason before they went in to bat. We wished them luck and they set off for the middle.

The first thing I noticed was that Sam Keeping, their captain and wicket-keeper, was standing up to the wicket for the opening bowler even though he was quite quick.

Liam Katz had warned me that Sam was good. But he wasn't good, he was brilliant. He nearly stumped Jason in the first over. Jason played forward to a widish ball down the leg side and Sam took it and had the bails off all in one movement. Jason still had the tip of his right toe on the line or he'd have been done for.

Our start was as slow as theirs. Their opening bowlers were called D'Anger and Woolf and, although they weren't as mean as their names, they were hard to score off. Erica and Jason were beginning to show the same understanding they'd had playing against the Berks. They were starting to pick up singles and they were running well between the wickets.

In the sixth over, though, Jason got a nasty ball from Woolf. It kept very low and hit him on the pads playing back. If he'd been going forwards he'd have had a chance but going back there was no argument – he was out lbw.

D'Anger struck in the next over. He bowled two half-volleys at Azzie which were dispatched like lightning through the covers. Then he bowled one which he held back slightly. Azzie didn't pick the slower ball and went to drive again; he played too early at it and lifted the ball to extra cover who took the catch.

21 for two after seven overs.

There was still a swagger about the way Clive walked to the wicket; he swung his bat round a couple of times above his shoulder and then slapped it against his pads. But at least he didn't tell us all how he was going to score fifty in ten minutes.

For the first couple of overs he received you would hardly have noticed him. He played little push shots for singles and watched the bowling very carefully. Then Henry Rossi came on to bowl. He bowled left-handed – just like he batted – quickish leg-cutters which were off-cutters to Clive. It was left-arm bowler against left-hand bat.

Clive watched the first three balls of the over like a hawk. The fourth he leaned into and lifted over the bowler's head for four. The next he played smartly off his legs for two and the last ball he swept all along the ground with the spin for two more. Suddenly the Glory Gardens's innings had come to life.

Erica was still playing carefully at the other end, trying to push singles and give Clive the strike. After twelve overs, we were on 42 for two. Clive had raced to 15 and Erica was on ten. We needed 35 runs off eight overs to win the Cup. With eight wickets remaining our chances weren't looking bad.

Then we had a terrible piece of bad luck, Clive drove powerfully at a straight half-volley. The bowler just got his fingers to the ball as it shot past him, ran on and cannoned

Clive plays the sweep to a good length ball.

into the stumps. Erica was backing up and she was run out by a yard.

It's probably the unluckiest way you can get out in cricket. Erica took it well, but I could see she was really disappointed when I passed her on my way to the wicket.

"Bad luck," I said.

"Yeah. Let's see you win it now," she said.

I played out a maiden over and then watched in horror as Clive danced down the wicket to the first ball of Henry Rossi's next over. He missed it completely and the stumping was just too easy. Erica's dismissal must have affected his concentration. He walked off muttering to himself. He'd scored 15 excellent runs – but it wasn't enough.

Suddenly it didn't look so simple. While Erica and Clive were going along at over five an over we looked bound to win. But now we had two new batsmen at the wicket. We still had some batting to come but I knew a lot depended on me to steady things down. And seeing Frankie making his way to the wicket didn't cheer me up.

There wasn't much you could say to Frankie about batting carefully. He either batted his usual way or got out. A streaky edge through the empty slip area got him off the mark. That reminded me that I hadn't scored yet.

I got a tempting long hop in the next over and pulled it for two. But the target was getting more and more difficult. We now needed 30 off five overs.

To make things worse, Frankie was completely 'done' by the keeper off the first ball of the next over. He swung at a quickish ball outside the off-stump and, slightly off balance, he was brilliantly stumped before he could get his bat down behind the crease.

Tylan played a good shot down the leg side for two and then, attempting the same stroke again, he got a very thin touch to the keeper who took it standing up only a couple of feet from the bat. Tylan was amazed and out.

Four wickets had gone down for seven runs. The Mudlarks were jumping up and down, congratulating Sam Keeping behind the stumps. Suddenly the game had turned around and they knew they were the favourites.

Cal arrived at the wicket and immediately a sort of calm returned. He walked up to me and grinned.

"Looks like it's a good idea to stay in your crease," he said.

"Exactly seven runs an over," I said.

"Genius!" he said. "So what's the plan?"

"Win," I said.

"Aye, aye, captain."

Henri Rossi was taken off with one over left to bowl. I pushed the new bowler for two between extra-cover and mid-off to bring up the fifty. Then I ran a single down to third-man. Cal played two defensive shots off the front foot and having got his eye in, cracked a three off the back foot, square on the off-side. A single off the last ball gave us the seven for the over.

21 to win off three overs.

"How's the finger holding up?" I asked Cal.

"Sore," said Cal. "But I'll survive."

The next ball lifted off a length and hit his glove high up on the bat handle. It was almost a catch to the keeper but he was probably put off by Cal's scream. He threw the bat down and walked away holding his hand.

I rushed up to him.

"Smack on the sausage," he said, pulling off his glove and looking at the swollen finger.

"Want to go off?" I asked.

"No fear."

But Cal's finger was now definitely affecting his batting. The next ball he played defensively, but took his right hand off as he played the shot and the ball lobbed up in the air to where silly mid-off would have been. Sam Keeping immediately brought a fielder up. Cal pushed a single through the empty slips with a one-handed tennis shot. I thought I'd better try and keep as much of the bowling as possible. A cover drive got us two. The next ball was pitched up on middle and leg and I played it backward of square-leg. We ran the first run fast and as I looked up the square-leg fielder was bending to pick up the ball. I called for a second run and just got home as Keeping took off the bails. If the throw had hit the stumps directly I would have been out.

One ball to go. I looked around to see where I could get a single to keep the bowling. There was a space at mid-wicket as well as through the slips. I got a good yorker and it was all I could do to dig it out. No run. Only five off the over. Now we needed 16 – eight an over!

Again Cal and I met in the middle of the wicket.

"Try another through the slips or a nudge on the leg side. I'll be backing up for a quick single."

"Okay," said Cal, his face was drained with the pain.

The first ball of the over was a wide. Good, an extra ball to us. Cal missed the next one down the leg side but managed to pad away the third for a leg-bye. Then I drove hard into the covers but it was a badly placed shot and it went straight to the fielder. We ran one. That gave Cal the strike again. He got a short ball which he cracked to the right of square-leg. As he played the shot he let out a cry of pain and dropped his bat. But we still ran two. Eleven to win; eight balls left. Cal pushed the next for a quick single past the silly mid-off. Then I received a shortish ball outside the off-stump. Crack! It was the perfect cut. The ball sped away to the boundary just backward of square. But the fielder at third-man raced around and stopped the four with a slide, picked up and threw in. We only got two from one of the best shots I'd ever played.

Sam Keeping brought back Rossi for the final over. I looked up at the score-board. Eight to win. I could see Frankie hopping from one foot to the other and Erica with her head in her hands, too nervous to watch. Sam took ages to position his field. He kept the silly mid-off and brought in a slip for Cal. All the other fielders were saving singles except for a deep square-leg. I told Cal to get the single. Wherever he hit it I'd run.

Rossi bowled a good length ball on leg stump. Cal shaped to play it round the corner one-handed but it turned, caught the outside edge and popped up on the off-side. The silly mid-off threw himself forward and took an unbelievable one-handed catch.

The Mudlarks went wild. They all rushed round the fielder and slapped him on the back. Cal walked off. As he passed me he just said, "Sorry."

He had nothing to be sorry about. We'd put on 20 in three overs and he'd batted really bravely.

"Well batted, mate," said one of the Mudlarks.

Marty arrived.

"Get your bat on it and run," I said.

He did. The ball rolled out only two metres on the leg side, but I was through for a single before any fielder had got near.

Seven off four balls. Singles weren't good enough. Sam moved one of the covers, mid-on and square-leg out to the boundary. So this was the field I had to face.

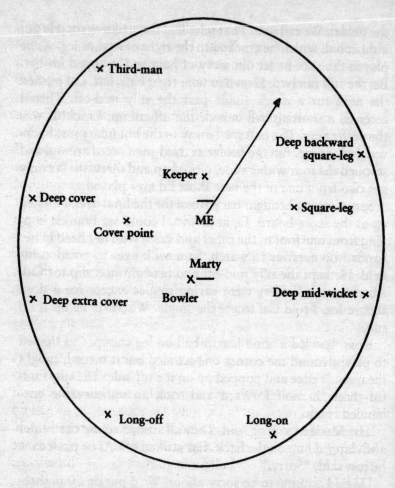

× Third-man

Deep backward
square-leg ×

Keeper ×

× Deep cover

× Square-leg

× ME
Cover point

Marty
×—
Bowler

Deep mid-wicket ×

× Deep extra cover

× Long-off

Long-on
×

It wasn't easy to see where I could score a two.

Rossi bowled on middle and leg. I knew there was a bit of
space at deep fine-leg, so I played a leg glance and ran. The
deep backward square-leg fielder ran after it. We got an easy
two but three would have been suicide. Five to win.

The next ball was short and I cracked it towards the leg side
boundary. But it went too close to square-leg, the only close-
in fielder on the leg side. He dived and stopped it. We ran a
quick single but I'd lost the strike.

Four runs needed from two balls. Marty took a deep breath and faced up to Henry Rossi. He swung hard at a ball just outside the off-stump and got an edge past the keeper but well to the left of third-man. We ran two very quick runs before the throw came in.

So it was all up to Marty. I didn't need to say anything to him. We needed two for a win. One would give us a tie, but neither of us were thinking of that. We wanted to win. I thought Marty would go for a big hit off the last ball and I got ready for the final sprint. If he missed we were finished because Sam Keeping was too good to fumble a run out. He took ages adjusting his field. The boundary fielders were brought in to make it more difficult for us to run two.

And then, at last, Rossi ran up and bowled. I was backing up half way down the wicket. It was a low full toss on the leg stump and Marty stepped back and cracked it. It was going for four over square-leg. We'd won. We'd won!

A huge cheer went up from the Glory Gardens supporters on the boundary.

And then suddenly an even bigger cheer from the Mudlarks players. What was going on? I looked at Marty. He was staring with his mouth open at his stumps. Then I saw it. One of the bails was missing. As I watched, Sam Keeping picked up the bail and held it above his head with a great cry of triumph.

Marty had touched the leg stump with his heel as he stepped back to pull the ball for four. He was out – hit wicket.

We'd lost by one run.

HOME TEAM	GLORY GARDENS	V	MUDLARKS	AWAY TEAM	AT EASTGATE PRIORY DATE JUNE 30TH

INNINGS OF... MUDLARKS .... TOSS WON BY MUD. WEATHER SUNNY.

BATSMAN	RUNS SCORED	HOW OUT	BOWLER	SCORE
1 B.WHITE	1·2·1·2·1·1·1·1·1·1	bowled	DAVIES	12
2 G.TUCKER	1·2·1·1·1·	ct LEAR	KNIGHT	6
3 H.ROSSI	2·1·1·1·2·1·1·1·2·2·1·1·2·4·1·2·2·4 2·1·1·3·1	bowled	DA COSTA	38
4 R.BLACKMORE		bowled	KNIGHT	0
5 T.KAYE		lbw	KNIGHT	0
6 K.ANDREWS	1·	ct ALLEN	LEAR	1
7 S.KEEPING	1·1·1·1·1·1·1	ct BENNETT	VELLACOTT	7
8 P.ATKINS	1·1·1·1·1	RUN	OUT	5
9 R.GEDGE	2·	ct BENNETT	DA COSTA	2
10 B.WOOLF		NOT	OUT	0
11 A.D'ANGER				

FALL OF WICKETS

	1	2	3	4	5	6	7	8	9	10
SCORE	15	57	38	38	57	67	75	76	76	
BAT NO	2	1	4	5	6	3	7	9	8	

BYES	1·
LBYES	1·
WIDES	1·1·1
NO BALLS	

| TOTAL EXTRAS | 5 |
| TOTAL FOR WKTS | 76 / 9 |

SCORE AT A GLANCE

BOWLING ANALYSIS ⊙ NO BALL + WIDE

BOWLER	1	2	3	4	5	6	7	8	9	10	11	12	13	OVS	MDS	RUNS	WKT
1 J.GUNN	··· ··1	2·· 1·	··· ·11	·· 1·2	X									4	0	9	0
2 M.LEAR	··1 ·2·	·· +·1·	X	1·w ·11	··1 ·1	X								4	0	11	1
3 H.KNIGHT	2·· ·1w	··· 11·	··· 111	·· w·w	X									4	0	9	3
4 E.DAVIES	111 11·	2+2 11·	2·· 4·1	X										3	0	21	1
5 C.SEBASTIEN	2·2 4·2	X												1	0	10	0
6 C.DA COSTA	3·· ··1	1·w ·1·	1·2· w··											3	0	9	2
7 T.VELLACOTT	111 11w													1	0	5	1
8																	
9																	

HOME TEAM	GLORY GARDENS	V	MUDLARKS	AWAY TEAM	AT EASTGATE PRIORY DATE JUNE 23rd

INNINGS OF GLORY GARDENS .... TOSS WON BY M.U.D. WEATHER SUNNY

BATSMAN	RUNS SCORED	HOW OUT	BOWLER	SCORE
1 J. PADGETT	1·1·1·2·1·1	lbw	WOOLF	7
2 E. DAVIES	1·1·1·1·1·1·1·1·1	RUN	OUT	10
3 A. NAZAR	2·2·2	ct BLACKMORE	D'ANGER	6
4 C. DA COSTA	1·1·1·4·2·2·1·1·2	st KEEPING	ROSSI	15
5 H. KNIGHT	2·2·1·2·2·1·2·2·1	NOT	OUT	15
6 F. ALLEN	1·1	ct KEEPING	GEDGE	2
7 T. VELLACOTT	2·	ct KEEPING	GEDGE	2
8 C. SEBASTIEN	3·1·2·1	ct WHITE	ROSSI	7
9 M. LEAR	1·2	hit wkt	ROSSI	3
10 J. GUNN				
11 P. BENNETT				

FALL OF WICKETS

	1	2	3	4	5	6	7	8	9	10
SCORE	14	21	42	42	47	44	69	75		
BAT NO	1	3	2	4	6	7	8	9		

BYES	ı·	1
L.BYES	1·1·1·1	4
WIDES	1·1·1·	3
NO BALLS		

TOTAL EXTRAS	8
TOTAL FOR	75
WKTS	8

SCORE AT A GLANCE

BOWLING ANALYSIS ⊙ NO BALL + WIDE																	
BOWLER	1	2	3	4	5	6	7	8	9	10	11	12	13	OVS	MDS	RUNS	WKT
1 A. D'ANGER	·:·ı	·ı·ı	·ı·ı	·ı·2 2W										4	0	12	1
2 B. WOOLF	·:·ı	·:·2 ı·ı	·:W ·:2	·ı·ı										4	0	8	1
3 P. ATKINS	ı·ı ı·:ı	ı·:ı	M	·:2 ı···										4	1	10	0
4 H. ROSSI	4·32·ı···	ı·:ı ı···	W··· ı···	W·2 12W										4	0	20	3
5 R. GEDGE	W··· 2W···	··ı·ı 22·												2	0	7	2
6 G. TUCKER	2ı· ·3·	4···ı 2ı2·												2	0	13	0
7																	
8																	
9																	

Chapter Sixteen

The Mudlarks were leaping about everywhere.

I walked down the wicket to where Marty was still standing and staring at his stumps. Sam Keeping rushed up to me.

"Great game," he said. "Best I've ever played in."

"Yeah," I tried to smile. "Well done."

"Tough way to lose," he said.

I put an arm around Marty's shoulder and we walked off without a word. As we approached the boundary, all the spectators clapped and Kiddo came up to us.

"That made me proud of you, kiddoes," he said.

"We lost," said Marty. And he added in a quiet voice, "Thanks to me." He was almost in tears.

"Rubbish," said Kiddo. "You all played like champions. It was the best game of cricket I've ever seen at the Priory."

It didn't matter what anyone said though. It felt rotten. We'd got so close to winning and there was nothing to show for it. I felt really sorry for Marty. I knew what he was going through. But he wasn't the only one.

"That was the worst shot I've ever played," said Azzie glumly.

"No worse than my bowling," said Erica. "I was rubbish. Look – seven runs an over."

Even Cal just sat on his own staring at his swollen finger and shaking his head. I'd never seen him look so fed up.

But the biggest surprise was Clive.

"It was my fault," he said. "First I run out Erica, then I play that crap shot. If anyone lost the game, it was me."

We were so surprised that no one said anything for a bit.

Then Frankie said, "Yeah, let's all blame Clive. After all, he only managed to be top scorer and take two for nine. So it must be his fault."

We laughed for the first time. And we started to feel a bit better.

Clive's aunt who'd been watching the match came over and she told Clive his batting reminded her of Sir Garfield Sobers.

"Don't say that," said Frankie. "He thinks he's better than him."

And Clive actually laughed. His aunt was really nice and jolly and some of it seemed to be rubbing off on Clive although don't go away with the idea he'd turned into a saint overnight – there was still a lot of rubbing to do.

My sister turned up and threw a crisp bag full of water at me. "Well caught, Captain Hook," she said. "Six runs to you." Suppose I couldn't really blame her.

By the time the presentation came round, we'd almost forgotten we'd lost. After Kiddo had handed over the Cup and the England bat to Sam Keeping, he produced a miniature bat, also signed by the England team, for 'the losing side in a great game'.

There was a big cheer from both teams when I went up to receive it.

"Three cheers for Glory Gardens," shouted Sam. And after their three cheers I called for three cheers for the Mudlarks. They'd been good opponents and if we had to lose to anyone I suppose I was glad it was them. Better than losing to Wyckham Wanderers anyway.

The 'Player of the Match' prize, a £10 book token went to Henry Rossi. And there was another prize for 'The Most Improved Cricketer in the Series'. Ohbert nearly fell over when his name was read out. No one argued with the choice. After all, when you start off as bad as Ohbert any improvement is a miracle. He turned to face us holding his book token and a huge grin spread from ear to ear.

"You'll be getting yourself a book on how to play cricket, will you, Ohbert?" said Frankie.

"He can't read," said Azzie.

"Oh but . . . you wait till next year," said Ohbert.

"Watch out, Hooker," said Cal. "I think he wants to be captain next season."

"Talking about next year, kiddoes," said Kiddo. "Did I tell you you were in the League?"

"Brilliant!" yelled Frankie. "Glory, Glory, we're in the League."

"It's going to be a tough season for you," said Kiddo. "It's the Under 13s League. So most of the teams you'll be playing will be a year older than you."

"We're in it, too," said Sam Keeping.

"Then we'll beat you next year," said Azzie.

"Beat them? We'll mash 'em," said Frankie.

And so ended Glory Gardens Cricket Club's first amazing season. Next year we were definitely going to win the League.

GLORY GARDENS C.C.

AVERAGES

Batting

	INNINGS	NOT OUT	TOTAL	BEST SCORE	AVERAGE
Clive	3	1	31	15	15.50
Azzie	5	0	65	29	13.00
Hooker	5	1	42	15*	10.50
Matt	5	1	37	18*	9.25
Erica	6	1	40	14	8.00
Cal	5	0	36	17	7.20
Jason	5	0	36	14	7.20

* signifies not out
30 runs to qualify

Bowling

	OVERS	MDNS	RUNS	WKTS	BB	AVERAGE
Hooker	14.4	1	44	8	3 for 9	5.50
Marty	16.3	2	48	8	4 for 7	6.00
Tylan	9.0	1	40	6	3 for 11	6.66
Cal	12.4	3	40	5	3 for 2	8.00

BB = best bowling performance
4 wickets to qualify

Catches

Ohbert	3
Frankie	3
Jason	3
Cal	2
Matt	2
Azzie	2
Marty	2

MATCH SUMMARIES

Friendly

Wyckham Wanderers (H)	Lost by 21 runs	
	Wyckham Wanderers	92 for 8
	Glory Gardens	71 for 9

Priory Cup

Birtly Parks (A)	Won by 4 runs	
	Glory Gardens	61 for 8
	Birtly Parks	57 all out

Stoneyheath & Stockton (H)	Match drawn – rain stopped play	
	Glory Gardens	75 for 3

Our Lady of Lourdes (A)	Lost by four wickets	
	Glory Gardens	23 all out
	Our Lady of Lourdes	24 for 6

Wyckham Wanderers (A)	Won by 25 runs	
	Glory Gardens	100 for 8
	Wyckham Wanderers	75 all out
Mudlarks	Lost by one run	
	Mudlarks	76 for 9
	Glory Gardens	75 for 8

CRICKET COMMENTARY

THE CRICKET PITCH

crease

At each end of the wicket the crease is marked out in white paint like this:

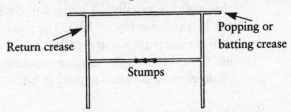

Popping or batting crease

Return crease

Stumps

The batsman is 'in his ground' when his bat or either foot are behind the batting or 'popping' crease. He can only be given out 'stumped' or 'run out' if he is outside the crease.

The bowler must not put his front foot down beyond the popping crease when he bowls. And his back foot must be inside the return crease. If he breaks these rules the umpire will call a 'no ball'.

leg side/
off-side

The cricket pitch is divided down the middle. Everything on the side of the batsman's legs is called the 'leg side' or 'on side' and the other side is called the 'off-side'.

Remember, when a left-handed bat is batting, his legs are on the other side. So leg side and off-side switch round.

leg stump

Three stumps and two bails make up each wicket. The 'leg stump' is on the same side as the batsman's legs. Next to it is the 'middle stump' and then the 'off-stump'.

off/on side	See **leg side**
off-stump	See **leg stump**
pitch	The 'pitch' is the area between the two wickets. It is 22 yards long from wicket to wicket (although it's usually 20 yards for Under 11s and 21 yards for Under 13s). The grass on the pitch is closely mown and rolled flat. Just to make things confusing, sometimes the whole ground is called a 'cricket pitch'.
square	The area in the centre of the ground where the strips are.
strip	Another name for the pitch. They are called strips because there are several pitches side by side on the square. A different one is used for each match.
track	Another name for the pitch or strip.
wicket	'Wicket' means two things, so it can sometimes confuse people. 1 The stumps and bails at each end of the pitch. The batsman defends his wicket. 2 The pitch itself. So you can talk about a hard wicket or a turning wicket (if it's taking spin).

BATTING

attacking strokes	The attacking strokes in cricket all have names. There are forward strokes (played off the front foot) and backward strokes (played

140

off the back foot). The drawing shows where the different strokes are played around the wicket.

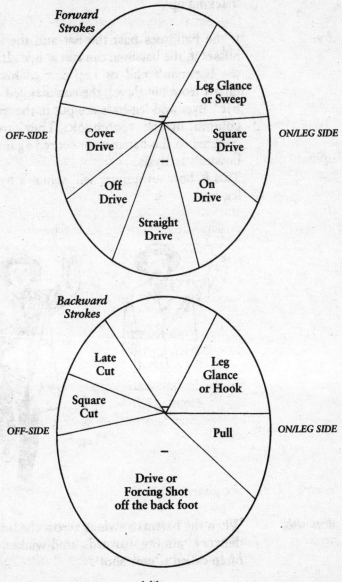

Forward Strokes

Leg Glance or Sweep

Cover Drive

Square Drive

Off Drive

On Drive

Straight Drive

OFF-SIDE

ON/LEG SIDE

Backward Strokes

Late Cut

Leg Glance or Hook

Square Cut

Pull

OFF-SIDE

ON/LEG SIDE

Drive or Forcing Shot off the back foot

backing up	As the bowler bowls, the non-striking batsman should start moving down the wicket to be ready to run a quick single. This is called 'backing up'.
bye	If the ball goes past the bat and the keeper misses it, the batsmen can run a 'bye'. If it hits the batsman's pad or any part of his body (apart from his glove), the run is called a 'leg-bye'. Byes and leg-byes are put in the 'Extras' column in the scorebook. They are not credited to the batsman or scored against the bowler's analysis. This is how an umpire will signal a bye and leg-bye.

Bye

Leg-bye

centre	See **guard**
cow shot	When the batsman swings across the line of a delivery, aiming towards mid-wicket, it is often called a 'cow shot'.

142

defensive strokes	There are basically two defensive shots: the 'forward defensive', played off the front foot (see page 72) and the 'backward defensive' played off the back foot (see page 73).
duck	When a batsman is out before scoring any runs it's called a 'duck'. If he's out first ball for nought it's a 'golden duck'.
gate	If a batsman is bowled after the ball has passed between his bat and pads it is sometimes described as being bowled 'through the gate'.
hit wicket	If the batsman knocks off a bail with his bat or any part of his body when the ball is in play, he is out 'hit wicket'.
lbw	Means leg before wicket. In fact a batsman can be given out lbw if the ball hits any part of his body and the umpire thinks it would have hit the stumps. There are two important extra things to remember about lbw: 1 If the ball pitches outside the leg stump and hits the batsman's pads it's not out – even if the ball would have hit the stumps. 2 If the ball pitches outside the off-stump and hits the pad outside the line, it's not out if the batsman is playing a shot. If he's not playing a shot he can still be given out. The drawing on page 29 explains this difficult rule more clearly.
guard	When you go in to bat the first thing you do is to 'take your guard'. You hold your bat sideways in front of the stumps and ask the

143

umpire to give you a guard. He'll show you which way to move the bat until it's in the right position.

The usual guards are 'leg stump' (sometimes called '1'); 'middle and leg' ('2') and 'centre' or 'middle' ('3').

innings	This means a batsman's stay at the wicket. 'It was the best *innings* I'd seen Azzie play.' But it can also mean the batting score of the whole team. 'In their first *innings* England scored 360.'
knock	Another word for a batsman's innings.
leg-bye	*See* **bye**
middle/ *middle and leg*	See **guard**
out	There are six common ways of a batsman being given out in cricket: bowled, caught, lbw, hit wicket, run out and stumped. Then there are a few rare ones like handled the ball and hit the ball twice. When the fielding side thinks the batsman is out they must appeal (usually a shout of "Owzthat"). If the umpire considers the batsman is out, he will signal 'out' like this:

play *forward/back*	You play forward by moving your front foot down the wicket towards the bowler as you play the ball. You play back by putting your weight on the back foot and leaning towards the wicket.

You play forward to well-pitched-up bowling and back to short-pitched bowling.

rabbit   Poor or tail-end batsman.

run   A run is scored when the batsman hits the ball and runs the length of the pitch. If he fails to reach the popping crease before the ball is thrown in and the bails are taken off, he is 'run out'. Four runs are scored when the ball is hit across the boundary. Six runs are scored when it crosses the boundary without bouncing.

This is how the umpire signals 'four' and 'six'.

four

six

If the batsman does not put his bat down inside the popping crease at the end of a run before setting off on another run, the umpire will signal 'one short' like this.

A run is then deducted from the total by the scorer.

stance	The stance is the way a batsman stands and holds his bat when he is waiting to receive a delivery. There are many different types of stance. For instance, 'side on', with the shoulder pointing down the wicket; 'square on', with the body turned towards the bowler; 'bat raised' and so on.
striker	The batsman who is receiving the bowling. The batsman at the other end is called the non-striker.
stumped	If you play and miss and the wicket-keeper knocks a bail off with the ball in his hands, you will be out 'stumped' if you are out of your crease.
ton	A century. One hundred runs scored by a batsman.

beamer   See **full toss**.

bouncer   The bowler pitches the ball very short and bowls it hard into the ground to get extra bounce and surprise the batsman. The ball will often reach the batsman at shoulder height or above. But you have to be a fast bowler to bowl a good bouncer. A slow bouncer is often called a 'long hop' and is easy to pull or cut for four.

full toss   A ball bowled which doesn't bounce before reaching the batsman is a full toss. Normally it's easy to score off a full toss, so it's considered a bad ball. A high full toss from a fast bowler is called a 'beamer'. It is very dangerous and should never be bowled deliberately.

googly   A 'googly' is an off-break bowled with a leg break action (see **leg break**) out of the back of the hand like this.

hat trick   Three wickets from three consecutive balls by one bowler. They don't have to be in the same over i.e. two wickets from the last two balls of one over and one from the first of the next.

half-volley   See **length**

leg break/   The 'leg break' is a delivery from a spinner
off-break   which turns from leg to off. An 'off-break'
                 turns from off to leg.

That's easy to remember when it's a right-
hand bowler bowling to a right-hand batsman. But when a right-arm, off-break bowler
bowls to a left-handed bat he is bowling leg-
breaks. And a left-hander bowling with an
off-break action bowls leg-breaks to a right-
hander. It takes some working out – but the
drawing helps.

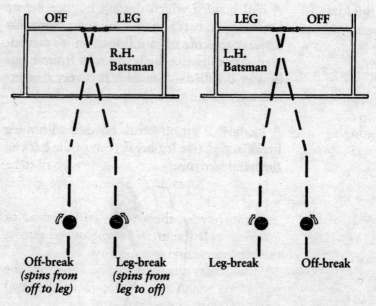

| OFF | LEG | | LEG | OFF |

R.H. Batsman   L.H. Batsman

Off-break   Leg-break   Leg-break   Off-break
(*spins from*   (*spins from*
off to leg)   *leg to off*)

leg-cutter/   A ball which cuts away off the pitch from leg
off-cutter   to off-leg is a 'leg-cutter'. The 'off-cutter' goes
                 from off to leg. Both these deliveries are
                 bowled by fast or medium-pace bowlers. See
                 seam bowling.

148

leggie	Slang for a leg-spin bowler.
length	You talk about the 'length' or 'pitch' of a ball bowled. A good length ball is one that makes the batsman unsure whether to play back or forward. A short-of-a-length ball pitches slightly closer to the bowler than a good length. A very short-pitched ball is called a 'long hop'. A 'half-volley' is an over-pitched ball which bounces just in front of the batsman and is easy to drive.
long hop	A ball which pitches very short. See **length**.
maiden over	If a bowler bowls an over without a single run being scored off the bat, it's called a 'maiden over'. It's still a maiden if there are byes or leg-byes but not if the bowler gives away a wide.
no ball	'No ball' can be called for many reasons. 1 The most common is when the bowler's front foot goes over the popping crease at the moment of delivery. It is also a no ball if he steps on or outside the return crease. See **crease**. 2 If the bowler throws the ball instead of bowling it. If the arm is straightened during the bowling action it is a throw. 3 If the bowler changes from bowling over the wicket to round the wicket (or vice versa) without telling the umpire. 4 If there are more than two fielders behind square on the leg side. (There are other fielding regulations with the limited overs game. For instance, the number of players who have to be within the circle.)

A batsman can't be out off a no ball, except run out. A penalty of one run (an experiment of two runs is being tried in county cricket) is added to the score and an extra ball must be bowled in the over. The umpire shouts 'no ball' and signals like this:

over the wicket	If a right-arm bowler delivers the ball from the right of the stumps i.e. with his bowling arm closest to the stumps, then he is bowling 'over the wicket'. If he bowls from the other side of the stumps he is bowling 'round the wicket'.
pace	The pace of the ball is the speed it is bowled at. A fast or pace bowler like Waqar Younis can bowl at speeds of up to 90 miles an hour. The different speeds of bowlers range from fast through medium to slow with in-between speeds like fast-medium and medium-fast (fast-medium is the faster).
pitch	See **length**.
round the wicket	See **over the wicket**

seam	The seam is the sewn, raised ridge which runs round a cricket ball.
seam bowling	Bowling – usually medium to fast – where the ball cuts into or away from the batsman off the seam.
spell	A 'spell' of bowling is the number of overs bowled in succession by a bowler. So if a bowler bowls six overs before being replaced by another bowler, he has bowled a spell of six overs.
swing bowling	A cricket ball can be bowled to swing through the air. It has to be bowled in a particular way to achieve this and one side of the ball must be polished and shiny. Which is why you always see fast bowlers shining the ball. An 'in-swinger' swings into the batsman's legs from the off-side. An 'out-swinger' swings away towards the slips.
trundler	A steady, medium-pace bowler who is not particularly good.
turn	Another word for spin. You can say 'the ball turned a long way' or 'it spun a long way'.
wicket maiden	An over when no run is scored off the bat and the bowler takes one wicket or more.
wide	If the ball is bowled too far down the leg side or the off-side for the batsman to reach (usually the edge of the return crease is the line umpires look for) it is called a 'wide'. One run is added to the score and an extra ball is

bowled in the over.

In limited overs cricket wides are given for balls closer to the stumps – any ball bowled down the leg side risks being called a wide in this sort of 'one-day' cricket.

This is how an umpire signals a wide.

yorker   A ball usually a fast one – bowled to bounce precisely under the batsman's bat. The most dangerous yorker is fired in fast towards the batsman's legs to hit leg stump.

FIELDING

backing up   A fielder backs up a throw to the wicket-keeper or bowler by making sure it doesn't go for overthrows. So when a throw comes in to the keeper, a fielder is positioned behind him to cover him if he misses it. Not to be confused with a *batsman* backing up.

chance   A catchable ball. So to miss a chance is the same as to drop a catch.

close/deep   Fielders are either placed close to the wicket (near the batsman) or in the deep or 'out-field' (near the boundary).

hole out	A slang expression for a batsman being caught. 'He holed out at mid-on.'
overthrow	If the ball is thrown to the keeper or the bowler's end and is misfielded allowing the batsmen to take extra runs, these are called 'overthrows'.
silly	A fielding position very close to the batsman and in front of the wicket e.g. silly mid-on.
sledging	Using abusive language and swearing at a batsman to put him off. A slang expression – first used in Australia.
square	Fielders 'square' of the wicket are on a line with the batsman on either side of the wicket. If they are fielding further back from this line, they are 'behind square' or 'backward of square'; if they are fielding in front of the line i.e. closer to the bowler, they are 'in front of square' or 'forward of square'.
standing up/ standing back	The wicket-keeper 'stands up' to the stumps for slow bowlers. This means he takes his position immediately behind the stumps. For fast bowlers he stands well back – often several yards away for very quick bowlers. He may either stand up or back for medium-pace bowlers.

GENERAL WORDS

colts	County Colts teams are selected from the best young cricketers in the county at all ages from

Under 11 to Under 17. Junior league cricket is usually run by the County Colts Association.

under 11s/ 12s etc.   You qualify for an Under 11 team if you are 11 or under on September 1st prior to the cricket season. So if you're 12 but you were 11 on September 1st last year, you can play for the Under 11s.

———————— • ————————

FIELDING POSITIONS

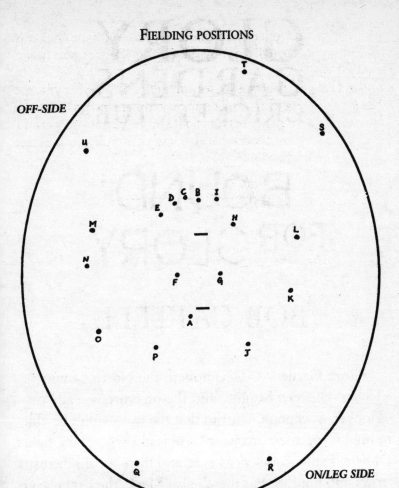

OFF-SIDE

ON/LEG SIDE

A BOWLER	L SQUARE-LEG
B WICKET-KEEPER	M POINT
C FIRST SLIP	N COVER POINT
D SECOND SLIP	O EXTRA COVER
E GULLY	P MID-OFF
F SILLY MID-OFF	Q LONG-OFF
G SILLY MID-ON	R LONG-ON
H BACKWARD SHORT LEG	S LONG-LEG
I LEG SLIP	T DEEP FINE-LEG
J MID-ON	U THIRD MAN
K MID-WICKET	

GLORY
GARDENS
CRICKET CLUB

BOUND
FOR GLORY

BOB CATTELL

Glory Gardens C.C. is now in the North County
Under Thirteen League, and the pressure is really on.
Hooker, as captain, worries that the team won't be able
to hold it together: arrogant Clive is always picking fights,
Ohbert is still as useless as ever, and there are all the usual
rows and injuries. But there's also Mack, the new player;
the lucky mascot, 'Gatting'; plus the whole team's
unwavering determination to win against
all the odds.

ISBN – 978 0 099 46121 0

RED FOX

£4.99

GLORY GARDENS
CRICKET CLUB

THE BIG
TEST

BOB CATTELL

It really doesn't look like being Hooker's season.
Not only does he spend the first match of the league
suffering a dropped-catch jinx but now there's civil
war in the team over the selections. Sometimes
captaining the Glory Gardens Cricket Team isn't
the fun you might think. It's not the matches that
prove the most trouble for poor Hooker – it's the
infighting. He has one solution that might work.
But making Ohbert captain in his place?
That's not strategy – that's suicide.

ISBN – 978 0 099 22342 9
RED FOX
£4.99

GLORY
GARDENS
CRICKET CLUB

WORLD CUP
FEVER

BOB CATTELL

Glory Gardens C.C. can't resist a challenge and this
time they're going for gold in a World Cup competition!
With teams from Barbados and South Africa visiting the
area at the same time, it's a brilliant opportunity for the
club to make its mark worldwide. It's not long before the
thrills and spills of cricket spark off sporting drama,
temper tantrums and practical jokes. So, as Australia
do battle with the West Indies and South Africa face
India, can Glory Gardens rise above the squabbling
and bring glory for England . . . ?

ISBN – 978 0 099 17842 2

RED FOX

£4.99

GLORY GARDENS CRICKET CLUB

LEAGUE OF CHAMPIONS

BOB CATTELL

GLORY GARDENS C.C. are back and this time the stakes are high as they play to win in the League of Champions! Hooker and co have got to get their act together fast if they're going to make it through the early rounds to the final of the knock-out competition. And let's face it, with Ohbert on the team it's not as straightforward as it might seem. As the competition progresses, the pressure builds and the team realise they are going to have to pull out all the stops if they want to make it all the way to the top . . . and Edgbaston!

ISBN – 978 0 099 72401 8

RED FOX

£4.99

GLORY GARDENS CRICKET CLUB

BLAZE OF GLORY

BOB CATTELL

GLORY GARDENS C.C. are Barbados bound for the cricket tour of a lifetime. Having begged, scrimped and saved for months they've finally got the cash together to take the team to the sunny Caribbean. Playing the top teams from the island, they find cricketing West Indian style rather tricky. What with rock-hard pitches and startlingly fast bowlers, if they don't seriously improve their form, it looks as if the Glory Gardens' players may have finally met their match . . .

ISBN – 978 0 099 72411 7

RED FOX

£4.99